LARGE PRINT F
Jones, Annie $29.99
Home To Stay
36968000016366   March 2012

9			
392			
1290			
~~583~~			
3194			

HOME TO STAY

This Large Print Book carries the
Seal of Approval of N.A.V.H.

HOME TO STAY

ANNIE JONES

THORNDIKE PRESS
A part of Gale, Cengage Learning

GALE
CENGAGE Learning·

Detroit • New York • San Francisco • New Haven, Conn • Waterville, Maine • London

GALE
CENGAGE Learning®

LIBRARY OF CONGRESS CATALOGING-IN-PUBLICATION DATA

Jones, Annie, 1957–
   Home to stay / by Annie Jones. — Large print ed.
     p. cm. — (Thorndike Press large print Christian fiction)
   ISBN-13: 978-1-4104-4273-4 (hardcover)
   ISBN-10: 1-4104-4273-X (hardcover)
   1. Veterinarians—Fiction. 2. Mothers and daughters—Fiction. 3. Large type books. I. Title.
PS3560.O45744H66 2011
813'.54—dc23   2011032336

Published in 2011 by arrangement with Harlequin Books S.A.

Printed in Mexico
1 2 3 4 5 6 7 15 14 13 12 11

But those who hope in the Lord
will renew their strength.
They will soar on wings like eagles;
they will run and not grow weary,
they will walk and not be faint.

— *Isaiah* 40:31

For Natalie and Patrick,
for being my inspirations and joy
For Bob for being my hero
For my family for being themselves,
and being my touchstone
For my by-marriage family for
being so much fun
For the next generation of "Joneses":
Ethan, Wyatt, Evie, Waylon
and whoever comes along next,
Aunt Annie and Uncle Bobby
love you always
(and will keep the toy closet stocked)

CHAPTER ONE

"If I'm not mistaken — and the twist in my gut tells me I'm not — that there —" Hank Corsaut fixed his eyes on a puff of dirt stirred up on the road a quarter of a mile in the distance "— is trouble."

The silver SUV went sailing over the bumps in the old dirt road that led from the highway to the sanctuary proper and disappeared down a hill.

Hank braced his hand against the dinged-up fender of his old truck and shifted his white straw cowboy hat to the back of his head. He had come out to check on things at the Gall Rive Migratory Bird Sanctuary this morning with all the good humor and enthusiasm of a feral tomcat facing a flea dip. He was a large-animal vet, after all, not a watchdog.

The car slid around the last long curve then went whisking by where he had pulled off to the side of the road without so much as the customary "hey, I see ya there" wave of her hand.

"Yep. That's trouble all right. Wavy-haired, heart-stompin', stubborn-as-she-is-beautiful trouble," he muttered.

This new development was doing nothing to brighten his mood.

Not that he had been particularly cheerful since Samantha Jolene Newberry, the woman who single-handedly ran the bird sanctuary and more often than not thought she ought to run Hank's life, had fainted dead away in his arms. *Dead away.* In this case it was not a colorful turn of phrase.

He wasn't sure for how long, but being a doctor of veterinary medicine he knew that when her body fell into his arms her heart had stopped beating. And Sammie Jo's being one of the biggest hearts he'd ever known, it had grieved him like nothing he'd ever experienced. Then her eyes opened again, and she let loose on him a whole new wave of grief — of the bossing him around, getting him to agree to do things he didn't have the time or inclination to do variety. He had had to agree to do her bidding before she'd let him call for help.

Hank rubbed his eyes, clenched his teeth and wondered what he was thinking when he had taken on the task. These acres of

10

untouched natural habitat swept with tall grasses, live oaks hung thick with moss, isolated with nothing but dirt roads to connect them to the highway and nearest neighbors, had withstood hurricanes and the high-strung females that lived here. What could happen in the few days Sammie Jo would have to be under a doctor's care as she recovered from her near brush with a heart attack?

The silver SUV didn't just make the turn into the drive that most people, even ones who had been out to the Newberry family home dozens of times, missed. It went gliding around the bend and through the crookedly hanging open iron gates like a plane coming in for a perfect landing.

Hank's feet seemed to grow roots, anchoring him in place. He'd pulled over just shy of Sammie Jo's yard to let the dogs run for a minute to expend some energy so the animals would be less inclined to chase any wounded or unsuspecting birds on the sanctuary proper. That's what he'd told himself. In truth he'd needed a moment alone with his thoughts, alone with the Lord, to regroup and go back to the place where not twelve hours ago he'd thought he'd lost one of the first people who had ever believed in him.

The SUV disappeared over a rise in the sparsely graveled drive.

What could happen while the owner was away? The past could come calling, that's what. Sammie Jo's past. Gall Rive's past. Hank's past.

All those pasts wrapped up in the form of Emma Evangeline Newberry, the girl who had run out on him on the eve of their elopement. He pressed his callused fingers against the pale blue oxidized paint of the truck until his skin burned.

If he got into that truck right now and drove until he got back to town or maybe even all the way back to New Orleans, where he had lived before he ever heard of the Newberry family, no one would blame him. But Sammie Jo had asked him to help out, and he had vowed to do it. Unlike some people he could think of — that he often thought of over the past ten years — he would not turn his back on someone just because things did not go according to the plan.

With a snap of his fingers, Hank directed his pair of rescued shelter dogs to get into the extended cab behind the seat.

"Gotta go, boys." He climbed in behind the steering wheel and slammed the door. "Looks like Emma Newberry has finally come home to Gall Rive. Let's go welcome her, shall we?"

Earnest T, a lanky, scruffy-looking Australian shepherd and Airedale mix, stuck his head between the seat and the passenger-side window and gave a gruff *woof.*

Hank cranked the engine and shifted into Drive. "Don't worry. I have no intention of getting involved with her."

A doctor of veterinary medicine for about a decade now, he didn't hold much with the idea some folks had of carrying on conversations with the creatures in the animal kingdom. Particularly when those people took it upon themselves to hold up both sides of that exchange as if they knew the minds of the animals themselves. But as a man who had landed wounded and weary in this small town hoping to put his lonely and painful childhood and family life behind him, he also embraced the notion that sometimes a man needed to think things out loud, to unload a bit to a sympathetic ear. All the better if that ear didn't have a direct connection to a pair of lips that might blab it all to the neighbors.

"No, I've learned my lesson as far as Emma Newberry is concerned," Hank said.

Otis, Earnest T's bulldog best buddy, snorted.

"I mean it." He pulled the old truck onto the well-rutted road and headed after the SUV. "I won't give her the chance to get to me again. Not that she would be interested . . . She made that perfectly clear when she left me without even saying good-bye."

The truck hit a dip in the road. The dogs bounced into each other. Earnest T laid his ears back and gave Hank a look someone else might have described as scolding. Otis lapped his tongue out and slobbered.

"Almost there, right through these trees, boys." He wasn't talking to the dogs, he justified inwardly. He was talking . . . to keep from thinking about what waited for him through those trees, what had his pulse racing and his mouth dry. He eased out a long, resigned breath then gripped the steering wheel to maintain control over the last bit of broken road.

Up ahead sat the silver SUV framed by a yard scattered with live oaks. Hank thought the moss hanging from their branches looked like streamers, as if the very landscape had arranged itself to welcome home this too-long-absent member of the family.

Movement in the driver's seat drew his attention, but the SUV's tinted windows kept him from seeing the driver clearly. He

14

reached across the seat of his truck to the passenger-side door and yanked the handle. When she opened her door, he would call out to her. Better that than jumping out of a truck and striding up to her. He was only thinking of *her* feelings.

Which meant he had completely forgotten to take into account his dogs' eagerness to get out and get an eyeful and a snout full of Gall Rive's newest arrival.

As soon as the passenger door of his truck came open just a crack, Earnest T gave Hank's elbow a hard nudge. The truck door swung outward. The already banged-up truck door went clanging into the cautiously opening door of the SUV just a few feet away. The wham of metal against metal rang in the quiet of the slowly spreading daylight.

Earnest T leaped out.

Otis came clumping along after.

A flurry of waves of rich brown hair whipped forward and back from the SUV's open door. The lower part of a tanned leg kicked outward. A high-heeled shoe went somersaulting into the shaggy, damp grass. A glimpse of black fabric, a flash of something shiny and a hand grasping nothing but air. That was all Hank saw of her.

That was enough.

His heart lodged in his throat, sending a

hard, expectant pounding beat all the way to his temples.

She let out a sound that, as a vet, Hank was prone to call a yelp followed by a series of unfinished thoughts that went something like, "My car! Dogs? Where did . . . This is my family's property . . . Keep these vicious animals . . ."

At that point she lunged from her seat to grab the door handle. That was her first mistake.

She leaned out and down and right into the path of Earnest T's ice-cold nose, extended in the enthusiastic reverie of doggy greeting. Otis's unfurled ribbon of a tongue was not far behind.

"Yeah, they are pretty vicious." Hank laughed. "That one licked the scowl right off your face. If you're not careful one of them might actually get you to smile."

Earnest T and Otis went loping back and forth, sniffing at the tires and underside of the new vehicle.

As soon as they moved away from her, Emma jerked her head up. Her hair bunched against her slender neck and over her bare upper arm but mostly it covered her eyes.

Hank could hardly see her face, or anything but bits of her — a bare foot, an arm, the wink of gold and diamonds on her wrist. Still, just being this close to her made something in him feel suddenly . . .

Lighter? Not exactly.

Love struck? Hardly.

As if he'd come home.

He pushed the fleeting and foolish thought aside. Closed the lid on it. Locked it down. That's how he had survived his childhood, how he dealt with the hard realities of his work, how he had coped all those years ago when this very woman had broken his heart.

"This is private property. You should take your dogs and get off it before I call . . ." Emma pushed the tangle of hair back from her face with one hand, lifted her chin and her gaze met his. "You."

"No need to call me, Emma. I'm already here." Had he thought she felt like home? Hank got out of the truck. He should have been suspicious at the tenderness and warmth he'd associated with the term. Those things had nothing to do with the home he'd grown up in. Maybe there was more warning than welcome in his first thoughts about the youngest Newberry.

The dogs rounded the SUV and headed for Emma again.

Hank strode to the back of his truck to better take command of the situation — at least the situation with his dogs. He had not quite gotten between the two vehicles when a squeal of pure delight caught his attention.

Layers of pink-netting stuff flipped and flapped and fluttered above the tops of clunky green rubber boots that were clomping over the overgrown grass of the yard. A purple knit scarf bounced over the orange-and-yellow swirls of a tie-dyed T-shirt. A small girl with tufts of blond hair sticking up here and there on her head stumbled over Emma's lost shoe. Arms flung wide she shrieked, "Dog-friends! Dog-friends! Here I am! I want to hug you, dog-friends."

"Ruthie, no!" Emma's arm shot out, but between Earnest T and Otis and her own safety belt restraining her she couldn't climb out of the driver's seat fast enough. "You don't know these dogs. They might bite you."

Hank clenched his jaw at her frantic tone, knowing it was doing nothing to calm the dogs or educate the child. He stepped in front of the girl rushing headlong toward the animals who had spotted her and turned to bound her way. He gave a quick, sharp whistle, held out his hand and said, "Cool it."

The child pulled up short in her tracks.

"You have no right to yell at my daughter." The click and clatter of the seat belt releasing underscored Emma's indignation.

"I wasn't yelling." Daughter? Emma Newberry had a *daughter?* Even without looking at the child's bright hair and pale skin or guessing from her slight build and barely-out-of-first-grade behavior, Hank knew the child was not his. That meant Emma had . . . married? He'd told Emma's aunt shortly after Emma left never to mention her to him again, and Sammie Jo had honored his wishes. Now he wished he'd have at least asked about the big stuff, marriage, children, that might have prepared him for this moment.

"I never yell." He adjusted his hat and tipped his head back, not quite making eye contact as he said, with as much quiet grace as he could muster, "And I wasn't talking to . . . your daughter."

He had no problem believing that Emma had become a mother, though. Not after the talk they had had the last night he had seen her.

He nodded toward Earnest T and Otis. "I was giving a command to my dogs."

Emma tipped her face down toward the pair of dogs lying in the grass between the vehicles with their expectant gazes trained on Hank. "Oh."

Hank bent at the knees to lower himself eye to eye with the child to better impart a little heart-to-heart lesson. "Your mom is right about running up to strange dogs, sweetheart. You should never do that. Not all dogs are your friends."

"All dogs are *my* friends," she said back at him, her tone decidedly stubborn as he might have expected of Emma's child. Still, something was off about the cadence . . . the sentiment . . . the "not quite connecting" of it all.

Hank studied the girl, carefully, methodically, which was pretty much how he approached everything and everyone. "I know you want to think that but —"

"There's no point in arguing with her." The distinct *swish-thump-swish* of Emma walking one-shoed up behind him alerted him to her closing in on him. "She's —"

"Yeah, I know." Hank held up his hand to cut her off. "She's a Newberry woman. And when a Newberry woman makes up her mind about something, then she expects the rest of the world to order itself according to her. . . ." He stood and turned to face her at last, prepared to see a cool, aloof, polished professional woman ready to fiercely protect her child. Instead he saw an almost frail figure with uncombed hair blowing in the breeze, dark circles blended with smudged makeup beneath her luminous eyes, wearing . . . "What are you wearing?"

"What?" She glanced down as her fingers flitted over one slender strap. She adjusted the sparkling belt then tugged at the hem just above her knees. "It's your basic little black dress. Every woman needs one."

"Not in Gall Rive." He shook his head. "And certainly not at a bird sanctuary at half-past dawn."

"You know us Newberry women. When you live your life expecting the world to bend to your every whim, you have to be prepared for anything." She pushed past him in a way that let him know that she neither appreciated his opinion of the women of her family nor was she inclined to explain her attire to him. She held her arms out to her child. "You never know when you might get an impromptu invite to a glam party."

"Obviously, *this* isn't one of those times," he joked in a way he hoped sounded casual not combative.

"Obviously." She stood there holding her daughter by the hand. Their eyes met for a moment. Color washed up over her warm-toned skin, rising into her cheeks and the

21

tip of her perfect nose.

There was that feeling deep in his gut again. The welcoming one, not the warning one. He didn't like it. Not one bit. And he didn't intend to endure it any longer than he had to. "Emma, I —"

"I'm sorry, Hank. I've been driving all night and I just . . ." She blinked and tears washed her eyes but did not fall.

That got to him in ways he was totally unprepared for. Still, he should say something. He wished he still knew her well enough not to have to say anything at all. He settled for a softly spoken "It's okay."

"No. It's not. I've acted like a brat, ordering you off the property without even asking . . ." She glanced down and suddenly seemed enthralled with something. She took a step, a lurch really, then bent and picked up the shoe that had flown off her foot when she had ordered him off the property. She held the elegant black pump up and turned it one way then another, as if trying to discern exactly what it was and what she should do with it. "Huh."

"I want that!" The little girl, her arms held up, fingers straining to wind around the slender heel, danced and leaped around her mom, who seemed to have completely zoned out.

"Emma? You okay?" he asked.

"Can I have your shoe, Mommy?" The girl tugged at the hem of Emma's too-chic black dress.

"When did that come off?" she said, relief easing over her pinched features. She laughed lightly. "I made it all the way from Atlanta in heels, survived pit stops for coffee to keep me awake and moving and snacks for Ruth. But as soon as I get to Gall Rive, I start falling apart!"

She looked better when she laughed, even at a shoe.

Hank rubbed the back of his neck, not exactly sure what to do next. "Look, if you need —"

"No. No. I'll be fine. I always am. I have to be, it's all on me, after all. Not like I have a choice. Unless, of course, I chose to accept . . ." She didn't even attempt to finish her thought, just looked down and swept her hand along the round cheek of the child beside her. Then she sighed, gave a wave of her shoe, bent to scoop up her child and began to walk away. "C'mon, sweetie, I don't know how much longer I can stay upright. I am totally exhausted. Let's go inside."

Hank watched her go, not sure what to do. Something was not right in all this, not right with Emma, not right with her child, not right with her showing up now and not asking about Sammie Jo. She *had* come back because her sister, Claire, had called her about their aunt, right? Hank had assumed, but . . .

"Buh-bye, dog-friends. Come see me some more soon." The child waved over her mother's shoulder.

Like her mama, the little girl got to him on some level Hank couldn't quite yet explain. "Why is she here, boys? Did she come for her aunt or is she looking for something?"

Earnest T whined.

Hank knew that was the dog's way of reminding him they were still in their "stay" positions and would very much like to get up and romp after the pair of strangers. Hank kind of knew how the animal felt in that respect. He wanted to follow them, not to just let them go off and try to sort whatever was going on with them alone.

Emma walked with an uneven gait as she made her way toward the large old house that sat at the center of the migratory-bird sanctuary. Then, just as suddenly as she had taken off, she stopped and called out, "Did I ask you why you're here? I don't —" she gave out a huge yawn "— think I did. Do you, um, did you need something?"

I need to get away from here, process a few things, he thought. What he said was, "I came as a favor to your aunt."

"Oh. Yeah. Not like you'd be here for me. Not like I told anyone I was coming home." She took another staggering step toward the house. Her daughter waved the shoe around and hit her mother lightly along the side of her head. Emma didn't even seem to notice. Another yawn. *"Home."*

Something changed about her as she said the word. The angle of her shoulders eased. She pushed one hand back through her hair and laid her cheek against her squirming child's head as she whispered, "You hear that, Ruth? We've come home."

As much as he knew he should turn and go, the awe in her voice, the tenderness of seeing the only woman he had ever loved as a mother drew him closer. He cleared his throat. "Been a while, huh?"

She shifted her weight to put herself facing the Newberry home again. "Funny, up until I decided to come back here, I had stopped thinking of it like that. It became a memory. Not quite real. Just a place I thought of the way I first saw it — like a big birthday cake on cinder blocks."

Built sturdy and adorned delicately, the

lower story of the house was gray stone. It had a flat, concrete downstairs porch jutting out into the yard and a broad outdoor staircase sweeping upward to the second story. That story had tall windows framed by faded black shutters against once-crisp white siding. The stair railings and the balcony were scrolled wrought iron, currently painted a dusty-rose color. Above that the dormered windows of the attic looked out on every side over the pale gray roof.

"I'd forgotten you'd called it that." Hank chuckled quietly. "Birthday cake."

"Cake!" The child lifted her arms stiffly toward the structure.

"Don't mention food, honey. I haven't eaten since lunch yesterday. I'm getting light-headed just thinking about cake." Emma settled the girl on the ground and put her hand to her flat stomach. She turned toward Hank again. She tipped her head to one side as if she had just turned around and noticed his arrival. She let out a long sigh before whispering, "Hi, Hank. I don't think I actually said that yet, did I?"

"Hi, Emma." For an instant the years fell away. She was fresh out of nursing college and he was still brand-spanking-new to his veterinary practice and anything seemed possible.

26

The little girl loped the last few steps up the walk and up to the huge double doors on the first floor. As her small fist pounded away, she called out, "Hello. Come out, Great-aunt Sammie. It's your pretty-great Ruth. I came to visit you."

"Visit?" That yanked Hank back to the present. He looked from the child to Emma. "Then . . . you don't know?"

"Know what?" Emma lifted her hair off the graceful curve of her collarbone and met his gaze unflinchingly.

"Your aunt Sammie isn't going to come out, Emma. She had a heart scare last night."

"A heart *scare?*" Her hand dropped from her neck to form a fist against her wrinkled black dress. She took a step in his direction, but her legs seemed unsteady. Her face went pale. Her voice barely rose above a whisper. "You mean a heart attack?"

"*Not* a heart attack." He took another step toward her. "I was here when it happened, she just —"

"No one called me." She seemed to teeter a bit, swaying but not actually moving her feet. "Is she . . . is she going to be all right?"

Another step and he was close enough to see the crinkles of concern between her eyebrows.

"Just a scare," he assured her. She looked in no condition to hear the details of the story from him right now. "Doctor wanted her to stay in town for a day or two as a precaution. That's all. That's straight from your sister Claire's mouth and you know she's not one to sugarcoat anything."

"I had my phone off while I was driving. Drove all night, after . . . I just had to get away and . . ." Emma put her hand to her temple. "I'm so tired and hungry. This is so . . . I came here because I couldn't . . ." She glanced down at her daughter and shook her head. "I thought Sammie would be here to . . . I thought Sammie Jo would *always* be here, and now you're telling me . . ."

He thought she was going to sit down, bury her head in her hands and sob uncontrollably.

Injured animals he could deal with. But crying women were way outside his comfort zone. And Emma, the woman he had thought of all these years as made of stone, dissolving into tears? "Why don't I let you into the house. You can lie down a minute and — I'll fix you something to eat then —"

"Lying down. Eating. They both sound so good." She put her hand to her head and yawned again. "I can't think straight but I need to talk to my aunt, or my sister or . . ." She took a step toward the house, pressed one hand to her head and another to her stomach. Her knees crumpled beneath her.

"Are you kidding me?" In less than a heartbeat he dropped his reservations about getting involved, his reservations about all things Emma, and did what needed to be done. "What's with you Newberry women and fainting?"

She didn't say a word as he fit his arm under the crook of her knees and wrapped his other arm firmly around her shoulders.

Her eyelids fluttered slightly.

"At least I know you're alive," he murmured as he jostled her around until he felt sure he had her securely in his grasp.

"Hey!" She roused slightly and tried to kick. The feeble attempt only emphasized how weak she was from her long drive. "Put me down. I can do this myself. I do everything myself."

"Nope. Sorry, not this time." He clutched her high against his chest and gazed at her sweet, sleepy face. "I have a key to this place and have already cleared my schedule for the morning. I'm going to watch your daughter and you're going to take a nap . . ."

"I'm fine." Her kick turned into more of a

halfhearted swing of one leg. She yawned. "I need to go see Sammie Jo."

"Sammie Jo is fine." It was nothing for him to carry her, even over the largely unkempt ground of the old bird-sanctuary lawn. He had made his living mostly wrangling farm animals, wrestling with everything from birthing cattle to giving a ferret nose drops. He could handle one wily but weary Newberry woman without any complications. "You just need to —"

"Be careful. That's my mommy," the girl said, her chin thrust out and her soft blond hair wafting in the breeze.

"I know. She's . . ." Hank looked down at Emma Newberry, who had laid her head against his shoulder when he'd begun walking. She was now blissfully dozing on his blue work shirt.

"Your mom is going to take a nap. But that's okay. You have Earnest T and Otis and me to look after you until she wakes up."

No complications? Her daughter couldn't be left to her own devices, her aunt was ill and her sister was preoccupied, to say the least. He hadn't wanted to get involved but he didn't have any choice. Emma Newberry didn't have anyone but him.

Trouble? Hank had a feeling that was an

understatement for what had just come home to roost.

CHAPTER TWO

"It's pretend cake, Ruth. This isn't my house. You aren't my kid. I can't feed you real cake. That's just the way it is."

At the sound of a man's voice holding a potentially temper-tantrum-inducing conversation with her daughter, Emma sat bolt up and almost tumbled off the edge of the couch.

Her mind raced back frantically over the events of the past twenty-four hours. She tugged at the neckline of her only really nice dress then ran her fingers over her diamond bracelet. She never should have accepted it as a birthday gift from her boss, Dr. Ben Weaver. She had told him it was too expensive, not to mention impractical for her as a nurse and single mom. But he'd made her feel like an ingrate for refusing the gesture. He liked to see her happy, to give her nice things, he'd said. That decision lead to another date and then another. And then last night, an out-of-the-blue proposal.

Emma shut her eyes. Why hadn't she just said no? Running away wasn't an answer. She of all people should know that.

"I think you'll find, Miss Ruth Newberry, that there is a lot to be said for having pretend cake. Starting with not having to do dishes after eating it."

Emma swept her gaze over the cluttered but homey living room of the old Newberry home and thoughts of Ben and the choice she had avoided making fell away. How did she get to this couch? How long had she been sleeping? And why was Hank — Mr. "kids are great — for other people" — Corsaut talking to *her* daughter about pretend cake?

"Ruth?" Emma pushed up to her feet and for a second the momentum made her head go woozy.

"But if you throw a fit —" Hank kept his tone matter-of-fact sounding, smooth and soothing "— you will upset Otis and Earnest T and the three of us will have to go have *our* tea somewhere else."

Emma pressed her fingertips to her temples and clenched her back teeth to force herself to focus. The room stopped swimming. She turned to find Ruth, still in her ballerina tutu and tie-dyed top, standing barefoot on a wooden kitchen chair painted banana-yellow, glaring across the 1950s' style dinette table at Hank.

Hank Corsaut! Her pulse kicked up. She couldn't catch her breath. She'd been too exhausted and too upset for it to really sink in earlier.

From the moment she'd run blindly out of one of the best restaurants in Atlanta, rushed to pick up Ruth and driven from Georgia to Louisiana without even stopping to change her clothes, Emma had prayed. She had prayed for guidance. She had prayed for insight. She had prayed for courage.

Maybe she should have prayed not to run into the last person she wanted to see at the old house on the same day she had come running home with her tail between her legs and her future up in the air.

"Cake," Ruth demanded with the quiet intensity of the calm before a storm.

"Sorry. No cake." Hank stretched his long legs out and did not budge. He did not even shift enough to make the somewhat rickety, wildly decorated wooden chair beneath him squawk. That impressed Emma, since she had painted those chairs herself more than a decade ago and knew how little it took to get them to complain under a person's weight.

The two big-eyed dogs, sitting in front of empty plates on chairs painted pink and lime green, watched solemnly. Silently.

Ruth did not show such grace. She gripped the back of her chair, her face beet-red, and let out a low, threatening growling sound.

Emma rounded the couch and headed for the kitchen. The soles of her bare feet slapped the warped boards of the hardwood floor as she said, "Hank, you don't understand. About Ruth —"

"I understand enough." He held his hand up to warn her to keep her distance. "If you want to talk to me about this, Ruth, you have to use words. Okay?"

Ruth shifted her weight from one fat little foot to the other. She frowned. She balled her small hand into a fist against the layers of pink netting of her outfit. After a moment she spread her fingers open wide and shook them the way someone might react to touching a hot iron. She didn't say a word, but then she also didn't grunt or growl, either.

Emma wanted to tell Hank that she considered this development a small triumph.

But before she could say anything, the

man smiled at Ruth warmly then nodded. "Okay. Looks like we have reached an agreement."

A shiver snaked up Emma's spine. Try as she might she could not look away from the man. Not even to keep him from seeing how much she found herself drawn to him with his easygoing approach, kind wit and seemingly endless patience coupled with unflinching sense of purpose. He wasn't bad to look at, either.

At thirty-seven his still-thick black hair did not show signs of graying. She couldn't say the same for her own dark brown locks at thirty-three. He still didn't seem inclined to get regular haircuts, though now the shaggy look seemed more a casual look than a young man too wrapped up in establishing his business to take time for the barber. His skin was tanned and he didn't show even the first bulge of a belly or suggestion of love handles.

The years had been good to him. He was no longer the kid she'd known and loved, the callow young man who had broken her heart by proposing to her and waiting until the eve of their marriage to tell her he didn't want children. Hank was a man now.

And she was a mom.

She could not let herself forget that.

She shut her eyes and made herself focus on the situation at hand. The familiar smells of the old kitchen eased into every nuance of her mind and memory. The ever-present hint in the air of Louisiana loam and moss and river grasses, of lemon oil used to polish all the wood in the old house intertwined with the scent of fresh cotton from all the kitchen linens aired on the clothesline. It all comforted her but did not blot out the image of Hank Corsaut in faded jeans and a denim work shirt, the sleeves rolled up to expose his well-muscled forearms.

Without even trying she could picture the watchfulness of his dark eyes, the way his hair fell against the beginning of smile lines fanning out above his high cheekbones. Whether climbing out of his truck coming to her aid or sitting in the kitchen playing tea party with her headstrong daughter, the man brought an instant sense of order to the chaos Emma seemed to drag along behind her wherever she went.

"Oh, Hank," she said almost like a sigh.

"What?" His masculine voice, with just a syllable, brought her straight into the moment again.

She pretended to rub sleep out of her eye and took a step in their direction. "Can I get you something for those plates and cups?"

"I unpacked your car for you and found the bag of snacks you had in there." Hank held up his hand. "So, we've eaten, thanks."

"Not cake," Ruth shot back.

"I explained about that," he said softly.

"She likes cake," Emma said with a soft, apologetic tone of affection she often used when trying to smooth her daughter's way in the world. "But if you want something to eat, I can look around and see if there's any —"

"Ruth asked Earnest T and Otis and me to have a tea party with her and we've had a very nice time sipping pink tea, which is pretend, by the way." He gave Emma a quick look, chin down, his dark eyes as somber as an undertaker's. Only the flicker of a smile gave away his good humor in the face of all he had been putting up with while she snoozed away who knew how much of the morning. "But when I suggested the boys might like some pretend cake to go with their pretend tea . . ."

Emma winced.

"I like cake," Ruth muttered.

One of the dogs woofed softly.

"Dogs like cake," Ruth added, more pouty now than agitated.

"But cake is not good for dogs." Hank held eye contact with the child, not an easy thing to do.

Ruth rocked from one foot to the other again. The chair wobbled. Her tutu swayed and rustled. She looked over at the dogs sitting at the table next to her then at the man treating her with dignity and yet demanding she show a level of discipline she couldn't always deliver.

She scrunched her mouth up on one side and lifted one foot slightly, which might have made anyone else seem off balance but somehow seemed to put Ruth at a cockeyed advantage. "Can dogs eat pretend cake?"

Hank had to tilt his head to keep eye contact, which he did. He managed a nod, as well. "I think that would be all right."

"Pretend *pink* cake?" Ruth threw it out almost as a challenge, as if she wasn't ready to believe the man had imagination enough to conjure up canine-safe and Ruth-approved pretend fare.

"Pretend pink cake with pretend pink icing on top." He lifted up what Emma could now see was an empty cup. "Shall we sip on it?"

Ruth mimicked his motion, reaching for her own cup, then paused to warn him, " 'Member your manners."

"Oh, sorry." With that, the rough-around-the-edges country vet delicately extended his pinkie finger.

Ruth did the same.

Hank raised the cup to his lips and made an obnoxiously loud slurping sound and that sent Ruth into a gale of giggles.

Emma's stomach clenched even as her heart warmed. She had come here to clear her head so she could make a decision about hers and Ruth's future. This was not helping that, but it seemed so good for her precious little girl. "Thank you, Hank — for everything."

"You're welcome." He set the cup down then turned toward her. "Get enough sleep?"

"No, but I think I'm recharged enough to go see my aunt." Emma stretched then yawned. Her dress rustled around her. "After I change, of course."

"I didn't think you were the kind to change for anyone." He looked at her then at Ruth, who was swirling her empty cup through the air while the dogs looked on. "Certainly looks like you went out and got what you wanted in life after we parted ways. I hope you and your husband are very happy, Em."

"I never married."

"Oh?" Again he looked at Ruth.

Her often obstinate child placed hats folded from newspapers on the head of one dog, then the other.

"I . . ." Emma didn't know how much she wanted to share with Hank about her choices and her life since she ran out on him all those years ago. Did he really need to know that she had never fallen truly in love with another man since him? Or that from the moment Emma had adopted Ruth straight out of the Neonatal Unit at the hospital where Emma had worked, until last year when she went to work for Dr. Ben Weaver, that Emma had put her child's needs first and foremost? Did he need to know how all of that tied in to her hasty flight home last night?

She opened her mouth, hoping just the right amount of information would spill out. Instead, her stomach gurgled. Loudly.

So loudly that both of the dogs looked startled. One of them woofed.

"You still aren't very good at the whole standing up for yourself and saying what you want, are you, Em?" Hank laughed. He stood and moved around to offer her his seat. "If you were hungry you should have said so, not asked me if I wanted something to eat."

She wanted to argue but she couldn't. She never had been able to put her own needs ahead of others. That was one of the reasons she felt so strongly about caring for Ruth by herself. It terrified her to think of even people who loved them both barging in with opinions and options that Emma feared might not be best for her fragile child. It humbled and touched her that after all these years Hank still knew her better than anyone, even than Ben, the man who said he loved her.

"Do you suppose Sammie Jo has anything but bird feed around this place?" Hank went to the nearly ancient aqua-blue refrigerator and tugged it open.

Emma sighed. She'd roused from a cold slumber thinking she needed to run to the aid of this poor out-of-his-depth man when he not only had everything under control, he actually wanted to help her. *If* she'd let him.

"Well, she has chickens so you know she has eggs." Emma settled into the chair and smiled at Ruth, who was busy trying to dab the corner of a napkin over the bulldog's lips. "I hope Ruth wasn't too much for you."

"Too-oo much," Ruth parroted, still trying to get all the pretend food off the face of the very real pooch.

"She was . . ." He set a bowl of brown and tan and white and even pale blue eggs on the counter. Then he turned around and honed his gaze in on Emma's face. "Surprising."

"In a good way?" Emma gave her fondest hope voice.

"She made those hats for the dogs all by herself" was the only answer he gave her.

"Yeah." Emma put her hand on the torn newspaper on the table, folded a corner down then tore the edges to form a two-inch-by-two-inch square, which she pushed toward Ruth. "She does that."

A moment later the smell of the gas burner being turned on high mingled with the aroma of bread browning in the old toaster.

"Over easy or scrambled?" Hank asked.

"Scrambled. Just like my life." Emma sat with her shoulders slumped forward. "I'm afraid with Aunt Sammie having this health scare, it might be lousy timing bringing Ruth here. I don't suppose you have an idea about that?"

He cracked an egg into the skillet, then another. As they bubbled quietly, he turned and seemed to study them both. "I guess that depends on *why* you brought her here."

She wasn't sure if the man was asking her

a question or suggesting she needed to ask that question of herself.

He went back to the eggs, gave them a stir. "What's she making, a teeny tiny hat?"

"Paper crane," Emma said, watching her child's fingers manipulate the square of newsprint. "There's a Japanese legend that says if you make a thousand of them, you can ask for one wish. I bet Ruth has made at least a thousand by now."

"That right?" He flipped the eggs over. The toast popped up. He got out a plate, slung a tea towel over his shoulder and asked, "So, what would you wish for, Ruth?"

"Crease." Ruth did not look up.

"Crease," Emma whispered, at last focusing every ounce of her attention and every emotion in her heart on her child.

Crease. It was the perfect word for the sound of Ruth's crescent-moon thumbnail sliding down the length of the folded piece of paper. The perfect word for the crisp edge left in that thumbnail's path. The perfect word for Emma's heart when she laid eyes on her child — folded in two, pressed down, forced into opposing segments, each cut off from the other but still whole, still Emma.

On one side there was all that she wanted for her child, all that any mother wants and hopes and dreams for her child. Opposing

44

that, the hard reality the world had dealt them.

"Wing!" Ruth proudly held up the half-finished bit of origami.

"Wing," Hank echoed in a tone that seemed in awe and yet not lacking concern. He set the plate of food down in front of Emma. "It's not fancy but . . ."

"It's all I need," she murmured, looking up into his eyes. "Thanks."

He shooed the dogs away from the table with a snap and a gesture. Emma wondered what this man couldn't do with those strong, capable hands that had held imaginary tea, cooked her meal, lifted her up in a moment of weakness.

He folded those hands in prayer.

Emma bowed her head.

"Thank You, Lord, for the bounty of life," he began softly. "Thank You for all that we have to eat, all that we have to share, all that we have to hope and for the gift of Your grace, Amen."

"Amen," Emma murmured.

He took the seat next to her, angled his shoulders back and folded his arms. "So, what's the deal with your daughter?"

She didn't know if he was asking why she had brought Ruth to Gall Rive or if he was curious about her medical diagnosis and story. But he was the first person she had ever met who had had the insight, courage and kindness to sit down and ask outright, so she told him the things that she had tucked deep in her heart. "Ruth can't say her whole alphabet. She still struggles to use a fork or a knife. When she dresses herself she usually tries, at least once, to force her head through an armhole."

He leaned forward, listening intently.

"When she does her hair, she usually rats it into little blond puff balls more than actually comb it. If the tangles aren't too bad, she puts a sparkly clip on them and looks up, smiling, for approval." Emma smiled, but it did not last long as she added, "If she gets angry about it, she pulls the clip out, and some of her hair with it."

"A lot of little kids —"

"She's eight years old."

"Eight?" He looked at Ruth, his head tipped. "Am I wrong in thinking she's small for her age?"

"She was a preemie." Emma looked at her daughter. Her heart filled with love and yet she still felt the twinge of hope and fear of all the nights she'd spent by the child's crib in the infant ICU, praying, singing to her softly, making plans for a nursery, a relationship, a life that she knew might never be realized. "I came to work at the hospital on the night she was born, took one look at four-hour-old Ruth with her oxygen tubes and terrified teenage birth mom who knew she couldn't possibly take care of a special-needs child and I knew I was looking at my baby."

Hank tipped his head to the right. He seemed to be making a study of Ruth but there was, in his expression, a gentleness and depth that he had never shown as a younger man.

That look warmed Emma's heart and yet made her uneasy at the same time. Rather than trying to sort out those conflicting emotions Emma took a bite and savored the simple goodness of her meal. "Mmm. There's nothing like farm-fresh eggs, eaten in a familiar kitchen, cooked by someone who . . ."

Someone who . . . cares about you? Someone you share a history with? Someone who let you walk away and never once tried to come after you, never tried to make amends? She stirred the eggs on the plate again, unable to finish that sentence.

He strummed his fingers on the tabletop, giving her time to conclude, then finally asked, "So you adopted as a single mother?"

"Eight years ago." She nodded, glad for

47

the distraction. "Aunt Sammie or Claire never told you?"

"I never talk to Claire about personal things. As for your aunt? I never asked." He laid his hands, palm up, on the table and lowered his gaze to them. "That first year after you'd gone when you didn't come back, not even for the holidays, I told Sammie Jo I didn't want to hear about you again. Not ever. I guess she got the message. And right or wrong, I just felt —"

"Bended." Ruth pressed down a pointed tip on the paper then moved to the final stage. "Pull, pull, pulled. Careful, it can still be broken."

"You said a mouthful, kid." He seemed transfixed by Ruth's fingers working over the tiny piece of paper. "She does this a lot, huh?"

She nodded. "She can't dress or feed herself without help. But this she *can* do. Folding and unfolding, creasing, pressing flat, turning, lining up, tucking in then opening up. You show her how to do it once, and . . ."

Ruth opened her hands to reveal her creation, an understatedly elegant origami bird. "Crane!"

"Very pretty." Hank held his hand out toward the girl.

"Too-oo much." She dropped the crane into his open palm.

"That about sums us up, I guess. Very pretty but too-oo much." Emma tried to smile.

Hank put his hand on her arm.

"Static encephalotrophy." She said the diagnosis out loud then followed up with, "Brain damage that won't get worse . . . or better. Same diagnosis as cerebral palsy, only Ruth's is less physical and more learning- and behavior-based."

"So you have to learn to work with what you have," he surmised.

"Not exactly the Newberry way, is it?" She bit into her toast and tore a corner off.

He sat back in his chair and chuckled. "No, I'd say the Newberry way is —"

"Who belongs to that SUV out there with the Georgia tags?" The front door went banging against the wall as Samantha Jo Newberry's rasping voice rang through both stories, each of the five bedrooms, down the hallways and most definitely into the big, open kitchen. "If it's a birder, I'm here to help. If it's my baby Emma come home at last, I'm here in the doorway with my arms open wondering how long I have to wait before I hobble in there, hunt you down and hug the stuffin' out of you!"

CHAPTER THREE

"Great-aunt Sammie!" The chair legs complained against the old floor as Ruth pushed
it away from the table. It almost tipped
backward.

"Whoa!" Hank caught it with one hand.

Emma darted her hand out to help her
daughter. Her hand landed firmly on top of
Hank's.

Ruth scrambled down off the tilted chair
unaware of either of them. "Great-aunt
Sammie. Great-aunt Sammie! It's me! It's
your pretty-great favorite kid, Ruthie!"

Emma watched her daughter lope away to
greet Sammie Jo. Emma should have
jumped up with equal enthusiasm and done
the same, but she couldn't seem to move.
All the importance of her rash rush to
return home settled over her. Hank, Ruth,
her aunt, her sister, Gall Rive, the past, the
future she had come here to contemplate
and everything they carried with them

50

settled like a mantle onto her shoulders.

Hank's dogs followed Ruth, their tags jingling rhythmically.

Emma returned her attention to Hank. She realized she had closed her hand over his, her grip tightening.

Hank did not shy away or even flinch at her touch. He met her gaze, his eyes kind but unrevealing as he asked a "safe" question. "Pretty-great kid?"

"The last time Sammie Jo came to visit us in Atlanta, we explained that she was Ruth's great-aunt, to which Ruth let it be known she was a pretty-great kid herself." A combination of love and recognition resounded from the foyer, with Sammie Jo laughing, dogs snuffing, their tags jangling and Ruth demanding to know where they kept the cake around this place. Emma managed an amenable smile. "It stuck."

"I can see why. The kid has a point." Hank settled Ruth's chair's legs onto the floor but did not withdraw his hand from beneath hers. "They are both pretty great."

Had she heard right? Hank Corsaut admitting he wasn't totally put off by a kid?

"Cake. Pink cake. Mom doesn't know where it is. My dog-friend's daddy doesn't know, either." Ruth's voice echoed a bit through the high-ceilinged house. "Come

51

get it for me."

Emma sighed and shut her eyes. It was all too much to process given her state of mind and the state of her life.

"You want cake? Then cake you shall have!" Sammie Jo's own voice rang out with a regal tone. "If I don't have any, we shall make one. Hang what the doctors say about diet and restricting cholesterol."

"Great, yes." Emma pulled back her shoulders and slipped her hand away from Hank's. She stood. "But she's also a very big responsibility."

"You talking about your daughter or your aunt Sammie Jo?" Hank grinned at her.

That grin gave her just the boost she needed to deal with the double trouble of her two most childlike and demanding relatives. She turned and headed toward the foyer, compelled to make one thing perfectly clear as she did. "Sammie Jo is my sister Claire's responsibility."

He stood up so quickly it made the table wobble and strode behind Emma, adding, "Except when Claire is busy."

"Which is, like, all the time, to hear her tell it," Emma chimed in, winding her way through the cluttered living room toward the front door where she could hear Ruth,

Sammie Jo and the pair of dogs scuffling around.

"Which is, like, all the time," Hank affirmed, keeping up with every sidestep and curve in the path Emma was blazing. "When Claire is busy, your aunt, and by extension, this sanctuary, has become *my* responsibility. Of course now that *you're* here —"

"No. Don't even finish that sentence." She pulled up short and spun on her heel.

"Give a guy a heads-up before you up and change course like that, will you?" Hank managed to stop just inches shy of slamming into her. He held his arms out and his hands up like a man trying to avoid brushing against a live electrical fence as he muttered, "Heads-up, right. Look who I'm talking to."

She tipped her chin up and narrowed her eyes. "If that's a veiled reference to our breakup, Hank, it needs to be very clear that *you* are the one that changed the course of our relationship. You are the one who waited until the night before our wedding to tell me that you did not want to have children."

"Really, Em? You want to launch into this *now?*" He retreated a step, his hands still up.

"I was actually sort of proud of myself for having held off this long," she shot back.

Before she could even take another breath, she cringed inwardly. She had made so many strides in life to keep her wild, impulsive tendencies under control, but standing back in this home of her childhood, after just a few minutes gazing into Hank Corsaut's eyes, and she was blurting out things like that. She pressed her lips together.

Another step back and Hank dropped his hands to his sides.

"I'm sorry." Emma hung her head, humbled by her own overreaction. "I probably made a big mistake even coming back here. I thought I'd find answers, that the path I need to take would become more clear with distance from my real life but —"

"Emma! My sweet, sweet, baby girl!" Sammie Jo appeared in the doorway from the foyer to the living room.

There was no evidence of a health problem in the rosy color of her cheeks. Her once strawberry blond hair, now streaked heavily with white, hung in a long thick braid over one shoulder. She had tucked her turquoise jeans into her high-top tennis shoes. Despite Ruth whirling about on tiptoe, her tutu bouncing and the dogs winding around Sammie's every lumbering, labored footstep, she entered the room like a diva commandeering the stage.

When all eyes focused on her, she threw her arms open wide, sending her hand-beaded dangly earrings swinging. "Look at you, all dressed up in that fabulous little black dress and . . . is that a diamond bracelet? *Très* chic! But your hair . . ."

"Note she's not surprised at what I'm wearing, just that my hair is mussed up a little." Emma went to her aunt, her arms open wide to wrap her in a hug.

"A little? Emma, honey, a little mussed up is what my hair was when I did a nosedive into the bougainvilleas." Sammie Jo enveloped her in two tanned, freckled arms.

Emma sank into warmth and the wonderful generosity of her aunt's unwavering love. This, she realized, was why she had come. She had been stressed, afraid and even in the middle of a crowded restaurant with a man who promised her everything any girl could ever want, she felt alone. Here, in this house, in the arms of the woman who had raised her when her mother died, all of that melted away. She was loved. And more than a bit curious. "You fell into the bougainvilleas?"

"Not on purpose, sugar. I was having a heart attack!"

Emma pulled away, her own heart racing. She twisted her neck to give Hank a scolding look. "You said it *wasn't* a heart attack."

"Oh, now, calm down, Emma, honey." Her aunt gave her one more brief hug before releasing her, stepping away and starting to pick her way over the tangle of dogs and Ruth. "It wasn't really a heart attack and I didn't actually fall into the bougainvilleas."

"I caught her." Hank leaned against the doorway, his arms folded.

"You make a habit of hanging around waiting for Newberrys to keel over?" Emma managed to keep her anxiety over her aunt's precarious health from making that sound like an accusation.

"I've just been telling everyone I had a near heart attack and fell into the bougainvilleas because it's so much more interesting a story than a medication mix-up inducing an episode that caused my heart to stop for maybe two, three seconds which wouldn't even have rated a call to the doctor if the town vet had minded his own business."

"You make yourself my business, woman, whether I like it or not." Hank shook his head.

"Boo-gun-veel-yas," Ruth sounded out slowly at first then began to spin around, repeating it faster and faster like the beat of a song that she alone could hear. "Boo-gun-veel-yas, boo-gun-veel-yas."

"That must have been awful for you, Aunt Sammie." Emma went to her aunt's side and took her by the arm. Sammie Jo nodded toward the couch and they headed that way, a bit more slowly than her aunt's usual speed.

"It *was* awful," Sammie agreed in her rich Louisiana accent. "And I would have been alone. Of course, God would have been with me — *is* with me, always — but I had my cell phone on me when I first started feeling poorly so I made a call and this one here —" she pointed to Hank in the same antagonistic attitude he'd been giving her but couldn't keep it up as she smiled, touched her fingers to her lips then blew a kiss to the man as she said "— came running."

Emma met Hank's gaze again, and again found herself overwhelmed by the sense that he could help her find order where now she mostly knew turmoil.

"The pair of them insisted I keep that phone near me and charged up at all times." Sammie Jo reached out to grab Hank by the arm as they passed him and her strong, slender fingers curled in a squeeze of obvious gratitude. "Of course, now that you've

57

come here to stay, that won't be such a worry."

"Stay?" Emma halted beside the couch and it seemed that for a split second everything around her blurred into slow motion, much as it had just before she fell asleep on her feet earlier. Only this time, it wasn't weariness that had her mind and heart out of sync with her surroundings. She had come to Gall Rive to test her wings, not to reestablish her roots. "Aunt Sammie, I didn't come home. I came back. There's a difference. I didn't come to stay."

"Like a bird who strays from his nest is a man who strays from his home." Sammie Jo dropped into the corner seat of the couch and motioned for Ruth to come sit beside her.

"What is that supposed to mean, Aunt Sammie?" Emma kept her tone sincere but she folded her arms for good measure. She knew her aunt too well to take anything at face value. The woman might be small and openhearted, but she was scrappy and used to getting her own way. Emma had stayed away for years to avoid her wishes and Sammie Jo's from clashing. "If it was a jab, you know I won't be guilted into staying here. And if it was just a flip remark, well, I won't be cajoled into it, either."

"Neither flip nor jab. It's from the Bible," Sammie said without looking at her niece.

"Proverbs, I think." Hank strode to the end table, picked up the large black leather Bible and thumbed through a few pages, then dragged the tip of his finger down one page. "Yep. *Proverbs* 27:7–9. 'He who is full loathes honey, but to the hungry even what is bitter tastes sweet. Like a bird that strays from its nest is a man who strays from his home. Perfume and incense bring joy to the heart and the pleasantness of one's friend springs from his earnest counsel.' "

He closed the Bible, laid it down and looked up to find Emma and her aunt staring at him.

"What?" He strode back across the room and looked down at Emma. "I teach Sunday school."

"To children?" She hadn't intended for that to sound so hopeful.

"To young adults," he said.

"Still . . ." She couldn't help smiling up at him. It was none of her business, of course, but the idea that this new Hank, actually this *older* Hank, was comfortable not just having a tea party with Ruth but taking a spiritual leadership role with people younger than himself made her heart cheerful.

"So, there you go." Sammie Jo struggled

to wrangle Ruth up into her lap.

The child wriggled free, protesting with a sound that spoke about her opinion of being held down more than a whole paragraph worth of eloquent vocabulary could. She made a spiral, went up on her toes and ran around the room repeating softly, "Boo-gun-veel-yas."

Emma did not have the luxury of grunts and temper fits to try to communicate her frustration to her aunt. So she went to the couch, settled on the arm next to Sammie Jo and asked without anger or malice, "There I go where? Unless you mean there I go back to Atlanta in a few days, I have no idea what you mean by that remark."

One of the dogs whimpered and raised his nose.

Hank turned toward the front of the house.

A creak came from the general direction of the kitchen.

"It's okay, boy," Hank said, scratching the larger of the two dogs behind the ear. "Just a kid looking for pink cake."

Emma exhaled then looped one arm around her aunt's slender shoulders. "So, to get back to the topic at hand, if there is anything you want me to know, Aunt Sammie, you are going to have to come right out and tell me."

Sammie Jo put her hand on Emma's knee and gave it a waggle. "What I am trying to tell you, child, is that just like the birds of the trees and the beasts of the fields —"

A car door slammed.

Sammie Jo startled.

Both dogs woofed.

Hank quieted them with a hand signal.

Too bad Emma didn't have something similar for her aunt. Sammie Jo lunged forward, using the arm of the chair and the leg of her niece to push herself to her feet.

She looked to the right, then to the left, then right at Emma. "Hide me! It's your sister!"

"Hide you . . . from Claire?" Emma stood partly to steady Sammie Jo and partly to try to get a glimpse at the front door through the foyer beyond the far end of the room. "You mean she didn't bring you out here?"

Sammie Jo started to move toward the kitchen. "Did you see her bring me here?"

Emma gave Hank a helpless look as she side shuffled along, trying to stay beside her aunt but keep the front door in her line of vision. "It's Claire. I assumed she was sitting out in the car running the world via her smartphone and satellites."

Sammie Jo paused in her slow progress

61

long enough to bark out a resounding, "Ha! Good one, honey."

"I'm not laughing." Hank came up behind them and put one hand on Emma's back and one hand on her aunt's. "But then, I've wanted to hide from your sister a time or two myself."

Emma did laugh. It felt good to have someone to help her deal with her family, almost as good as it felt to have Hank so near, the warmth of his hand sinking into the tense muscles between her world-weary shoulders.

"Hold it right there, Aunt Sammie." Claire Newberry burst through the door. "The doctor released you into *my* care and my care doesn't reach past the edge of . . . Emma?"

They had the same parents. The same upbringing. The same blue-green eyes and dark brown unruly hair. They had the same skin tone. Same height. Same bright intellect. Same faith. Same family frustrations. Same inability to fully forgive themselves for not being better able to love each other unconditionally.

Beyond that, they had nothing in common.

"Hello, Claire." She turned to face her sister.

"Why are you here?" Claire sighed. Dressed for the season in a denim skirt and white cotton shirt, both pressed and perfect, the older Newberry practically glided over the old floor as she came into the room. "I told you in my phone message that you didn't have to come."

"I haven't heard your message, Claire," Emma said softly as she helped their aunt sit down again.

Claire was at their aunt's side now, too, helping the woman who kept trying to bat away both of their well-meaning attempts. "I told you Aunt Sammie was fine."

"I'm sure you did." Emma clenched her jaw. Claire was too busy talking to hear a word Emma said. "But it didn't even occur to me she might not be fine when I started out last night."

"C'mon, y'all." Hank employed the same tone he had used to calm his dogs earlier.

Both sisters glared at him. Not the effect he had hoped for, she figured.

"I suppose, being a nurse you thought you'd be the best one to see to her recovery." She tugged at Sammie's arm. "Right?"

"No. No. Absolutely not." Emma eased her aunt's body away from Claire's grasp. "Listen to me, Claire."

"Girls!" Sammie put both hands up.

Hank leaned in, his hands extended. "Maybe you should just let your aunt —"

"No, you listen to me." Claire's gentle tugging turned to an insistent yank. "I have everything under control here. You did not have to come out here to save the day and by the looks of it straight from some fancy dinner with that doctor of yours."

"Girls?" Sammie wormed her arms from their hands and stepped away from them, her face colored with concern.

"Doctor?" Hank froze, his hand still out. He didn't take his eyes off Emma. "You have a doctor that you dress like that for?"

Defensiveness laced with a hint of delight coiled in Emma's chest to think that who she kept company with might matter to Hank. She opened her mouth to try to explain her situation, then closed it again.

"She has it all." Claire batted Emma's hand away from reaching for Sammie Jo again. "She knows it all, apparently, and can do it all. She can be a professional, a caregiver and a mom."

"Girls . . . please." Sammie Jo took a step away.

"Me? *I* know it all? I can do it all?" Emma pushed away Claire's hands, which had been batting away Emma's hands. They became a tangle of fingers and hands each

64

trying to shove the other aside. "Don't you have that backward? You're the one everyone counts on. I'm the flighty one, the impulsive one, the —"

"Girls! Hush!" Sammie spun around and faced the both of them. "I have a question for you that's more important than any of this petty sibling bickering."

"What?" Both girls asked at once, unable to pull their hands apart quickly enough.

Sammie put her hand on her hip and narrowed one eye. "Where is Ruth?"

For a fraction of a second everything went still. There was no chatter or foot stomping from Ruth. They all looked at each other.

Emma couldn't breathe.

"Ruth. Ruth? Ruth!" All their voices rose at once.

They all sprang into action. In a few ticks of the clock Claire began barking orders. "Hank, you and your dogs search outside. Emma, take the second floor and I'll check the basement."

"Good plan." Sammie Jo clapped her hands together. "That leaves the attic for me."

"No!" Claire's stern decree filled the house.

It did not slow Hank or Emma as they each headed for the foyer, Hank to take his dogs outside or Emma aimed for the stairway.

"You are not going up to the attic, Aunt Sammie," Claire went on.

"Someone has to. Remember how much you girls loved it up there? It's a kid magnet, that place, with all the stuff, that old tiny winding servant's stairway from the kitchen all the way up to —"

"The window!" Emma cried.

Her mind filled with the memory of sneaking up the back staircase past the second floor where all the bedrooms were and into the attic. She and Claire used to play hide-and-seek up there, then sit for hours on the sills of the old dormer windows and gaze out on the landscape and share their dreams of flying away. Since they didn't have screens Aunt Sammie had nailed them shut, but in later years as teens the sisters had pried at least one of them open so that they could climb out onto the roof and talk under the stars.

"I'm starting in the attic," Emma called over her shoulder to Claire only to round the top of the main stairway and come face-to-face with her sister, panting from having dashed up the back way.

"I'm coming with you," Claire said.

"You don't . . ."

"We'll have plenty of time to argue later."
Claire nabbed Emma's arm. And before
Emma could make it clear that she had not
come to Gall Rive to stay, Claire dragged
her sister toward the back stairs. "Let's find
Ruth."

The stairs groaned under the weight of
the four sets of feet running upward. As they
neared the open doorway to the attic, a soft
breeze wafting from above made Emma's
heart leap into her throat. "Ruth? Ruthie,
are you up there?"

"I can see the boo-gun-veel-ya from here."
The squawk of wood against wood, window
frame against window casing underscored
the strange claim.

"Ruth! Get away from that window."
Emma pushed ahead of her sister and burst
into the dusty old wood-framed attic to find
Ruth trying to pry the old window open
more than a few inches.

"I can see it!" Her tutu flounced as she
pressed one finger to the glass and twisted
her upper body around to face the doorway.
"I can see the boo-gun-veel-ya from here.
Can we go visit it?"

"Visit?" Emma hurried to the window and
scooped up her child. "You don't —"

"You think she means that great blue
heron on the pond?" Claire reached their

side, and pushed the window closed as she searched the landscape that included most of the bird-sanctuary property.

But when Emma moved to take a look, her gaze fell on Hank directing his dogs here and there, calling out to Ruth with the promise of tea parties and maybe even real cake.

"This window, in fact the whole attic, is off-limits, young lady." Claire took the child's chin in her hand. "I don't care how interesting you find that crane."

"Crane! I can make a crane!" Ruth spun around and headed for the stairway again. "I'll show you."

"Use the handrail on those steps, baby," Emma called after her child. When Ruth singsonged back something indistinguishable, Emma turned back to the view of Hank and sighed. "Things haven't changed around here. Never a dull moment."

"Oh, things have changed plenty." Claire came up beside her, gazed out into the distance, then at Emma, then down at the ground below where Aunt Sammie had made her way into the yard, with Ruth on her heels, to speak to Hank. "Stick around a while and you'll see just how much."

"I can't stick around," Emma said softly. What she really wanted to do was ask her

68

sister just what she meant by that cryptic remark, but thought better of it. No use stirring things up when she knew it wouldn't affect her reality — she wasn't going to stay. "I just came to Gall Rive to help me clear my head and figure out what's best for Ruth and me, what I really want to do with the rest of my life."

"Hmm. So, you came *here* for that?" Claire made a show of looking out and down to the man standing below them, trying to keep the circus that was Sammie Jo, Ruthie, Otis and Earnest T in check and looking very grown-up and handsome while doing it. "I hope you know what you're doing."

As Claire turned and walked away, Hank looked up to the window.

Emma let out a tiny gasp to have been caught staring at the man.

He smiled, waved, then pointed with his thumb over his shoulder toward his truck, letting her know he needed to get going.

Emma waved and mouthed the words *Thank you,* though she doubted he could see that.

A long, sharp whistle for his dogs and Hank started for the truck. He only paused to shake Ruthie's hand, a gesture she barely acknowledged in favor of showing her paper

crane to the dogs, who seemed more interested in tasting it than admiring it. In short
order the dogs were in the truck, Ruth was
in the care of Sammie Jo and Hank climbed
behind the wheel.

As he drove away, Emma leaned her
forehead against the glass of the old window.
She was mentally, physically and emotionally exhausted. She was overdressed, under-
rested and needed to spend the rest of this
day dealing with her aunt and sister, unpack
the few things she had thought to bring
along and find what she needed to beg or
borrow to get by. But first she needed to
find a hammer and nail and get this window
taken care of, then another nap to help her
get some focus back.

Too bad the issues that had prompted her
to make the all-night flight home weren't so
easily addressed. Ben Weaver wanted to
marry her. He wanted to take care of her
and to enable her to take care of Ruth in
whatever way Emma saw fit. And to top it
off he was willing to give her time to fall in
love with him. On the surface it seemed like
everything a struggling single mom could
ask for, but Emma kept thinking that maybe
what seemed good for Ruth might not be
what was best for the girl, or for Emma.
That wasn't the kind of problem she could

fix with a hammer and a nap.

Emma thought of her sister's response to Emma's claim she was only here to help find the right path to the future. *You came here for that? I hope you know what you're doing.*

"I do, too," Emma whispered as Hank's truck disappeared around a curve in the old road. "I do, too."

CHAPTER FOUR

His sense of responsibility motivated Hank to go out to the migratory-bird sanctuary the next morning. That's what he told himself. And that's what he kept trying to convince himself of — that he hadn't made the ten-mile drive from his home/vet clinic after his morning appointments because Emma Newberry kept dropping into his dreams and popping into his thoughts. He told himself that he hadn't come out here to try to make a connection with her, despite the realization that she looked perfectly at home even in an outfit that left no doubt that she had another life, a life of diamonds and doctors and dinner at places that were more than a notch above the handful of places to grab a bite and get the gossip around Gall Rive.

Just plain old-fashioned good Southern manners. That was what this was about. Sammie Jo had been ill. She had company from out of state. A good neighbor would pay a call.

Besides, the weather had taken a turn and the dark clouds in the distance boomed and rumbled with the threat of a pop-up thunderstorm. Those kinds of things were common around here in the heat of summer. With wind gusts that could blow down tree limbs, send small objects flying and, out here in the rural parts of the county, cause electrical blackouts that could take days to get repaired. With Sammie Jo away this past week and the house full, it seemed only the right thing to make sure they didn't need anything.

That's the motivation that spurred him to turn his truck toward the bird sanctuary. But when he crossed paths with Claire, Sammie Jo and Ruth heading into town, he had to see if Emma needed help taking care of things around the old place, right?

He told himself all this as he guided the truck off the road to the pond at the edge of the half acre behind the old Newberry house. Something entirely different coaxed him out of that truck when he stopped, though. He opened the truck door as thunder grumbled low from the not-too-distant west. Since he didn't have the dogs with him today, Hank left the door open so he wouldn't disturb the scene before him.

"I'm telling you this for your own good. Nobody wants you here." Her back to him, Emma Newberry pushed the weeds and rushes aside and moved with stealth, stalking the gangly-legged, gray-feathered bird that had taken to inhabiting the far side of the family pond. A bird that didn't seem the least bit impressed with her tactics or her attempts at persuasion. "You think it looks like a great place to settle down, but take it from someone who knows, nothing good can come of you hanging around this place."

Now that was the kind of remark a guy could read a lot into, he thought. *If* that guy were personally involved and not just "hanging around" to be polite.

"Shoo! Go! Git!" She popped her head up from the thick thatch of tall grass a few yards away and called across the expanse of glassy-smooth water. "You have wings, why don't you use them?"

As if to demonstrate to the wild creature, she raised both arms high then began to wave them up and down.

The crane lifted one leg then set it back again. It shook its head then cocked it, keeping one yellow eye always trained on Emma.

Hank couldn't take his eyes off her, either.

She was wearing bright pink jeans, obviously borrowed from Sammie Jo. Paired with the simple white shirt knotted in front and her hair done back in a loose braid, she looked . . .

"Flippity, flappity, flip! Take off!" She added jumping up and down to the arm flailing.

She looked like an adorable do-gooder who didn't have any idea what she was doing. Any minute now he expected her to start screeching or attempting to imitate the rough croaking cry of the large bird. He didn't know how much longer he could stand there without busting out laughing at her antics.

When she started to creep closer to the water's edge, raising her arms for another onslaught, Hank had to intervene. He planted his feet firmly on the bank and folded his arms. "I wouldn't do that if I were you."

"What?" Emma froze midflap. She spun around.

Their eyes locked.

"Hello, Emma."

The flush in her cheeks from all that moving around became a deeper pink. She dropped her arms to her sides. She stood perfectly still among the weeds and reeds as if she hoped she might suddenly blend in and become invisible. At last she cleared her throat and asked softly, "How long have you been standing there?"

"Long enough," he said, trying not to grin so big it might make her feel foolish.

"I was concentrating so hard I didn't even hear your truck." She crossed her own arms and gave him a pout that didn't make him one bit sorry he'd startled her. "You scared me!"

"That only seems fair. You're scaring me a little bit." He kept his chuckle under his breath as he took a step in her direction and extended his hand to help her up the embankment around the pond. He nodded toward the phlegmatic waterfowl. "Not sure you're doing that bird any favors, either."

"But that's exactly what I'm going for, doing the poor lost, lonely thing." She turned to him, glanced down at his hand then back at the bird again. "I'm doing it the biggest favor I can think of."

"Trying to give it a laugh with that little display of yours?" he suggested without withdrawing his silent encouragement for her to come with him.

"I guess I did look pretty silly." Again she looked at his hand then at the bird again.

He could hear the tender longing to do

what she thought was best in her voice. Her reluctance gave a tense angle to her shoulders that told him she needed a little nudge to abandon her ill-conceived scheme. "What exactly are you doing? You do realize that this place is still a bird *sanctuary,* right? The idea being it's a place where birds are *encouraged* to 'hang around.' "

"Not this one," she shot back so fast that Hank knew this was bigger than any one stray bird.

"They bite, you know," he said quietly.

"Bite?" She whipped her head around so quickly, it sent her braid bouncing over her bright white shirt.

"Well, they . . . could strike out, if provoked." He took a step downhill, toward her, never lowering his outstretched hand. "Ever hear of the fight-or-flight response?"

"Hear of it?" She reeled around and gave him a wry look. "I've been battling both urges every minute since Claire decided Sammie Jo didn't have to go back into town with her as long as I was at the house."

"Yeah. I heard about you getting elected resident caregiver until the doc says it's okay for Sammie Jo to be on her own again." Another step closer. Now his open hand waited just inches away from her. "That's why I came out to see if I could do anything to help."

She took a deep breath, held it, then slid her hand gently into his palm. "You really wanna help?"

He *really* wanted to help. He closed his fingers over hers for the first time in so many years. His chest ached. He looked down into her eyes and words failed him. He simply nodded.

"Then tell me how to get rid of that crane." She swung her arm out and pointed across the water toward the watchful bird.

The tightness in his chest eased. He dug his heels in to counterbalance pulling her up the incline. "Get rid of as in . . . ?"

"Make it go back to its family." She climbed with him to the road then looked back one more time. The breeze blew wisps of hair around over her temple but that didn't disguise the dampness in her eyes as she whispered, "They aren't meant to be alone, are they?"

Clearly this was not just about a wayward blue heron. He was tempted to draw her closer to him, to pull her into his embrace, lay his cheek against her head and to comfort her about whatever was weighing so heavy on her heart. He resisted the urge but did give her hand a squeeze. "Did you ever think it doesn't want to fly because it might be hurt or sick? Or maybe it's smart enough to know not to take off from a place it feels safe with bad weather brewing. Now, I'm no ornithologist, but —"

She let go of his hand and began to walk along the road in the direction of the old house. "Aunt Sammie Jo says to leave it be."

He thought of offering her a ride. But if she turned him down? Then what? He followed behind her on foot instead. "She is the specialist in that area."

"But it doesn't belong here."

He held his arms out to his side to indicate their surroundings. "It's a bird sanctuary."

She stopped in the middle of the road and spoke to him with her face in profile. "Okay, then I want it to go away, all right?"

"Any particular reason?" He had his own theories, of course. One was that Emma identified with that bird, showing up out of nowhere, without a flock or a mate, without any clear reason for being here. If she could get the great blue heron to take wing, it would help her feel that she could do the same.

"All right. I don't like it being here because now that Ruth has seen it out the window she keeps talking about it." The words rolled out of her almost on top of one another. Still, no matter how fast they tumbled from her, that didn't make them sound more believable. "You know, because she makes paper cranes and it's like a crane, she wants to get close to it. I just keep thinking of her being drawn out here wanting to make friends with that heron, and they bite, you said so yourself."

He shook his head, not buying it. "Ruth is not going to get close enough to a great blue heron for it to attack her."

"I'm also afraid wanting to see it will lure her up to the attic window." She pointed skyward. "That isn't safe any more than wanting to get out to this pond is. Making her way out here, the water, no other birds out here hold that kind of attraction for her, or pose that kind of threat."

"So you teach her not to go into the attic or out to the pond, or how to do it so it is safe. If you're concerned about her surroundings, you give her the tools to navigate them. Don't try to remove every possible problem, you can't do it. There will always be something dangerous, something she has to deal with." He looked around at them. "You can't bundle her up in bubble wrap and hope that keeps her safe. You have to teach her how to interact with her environment, how to make good choices, how to be smart, not scared."

Her lips moved to silently form the last phrase he had spoken before she scowled at him and asked, "Why did you say you came out here today?"

"To see if you needed any help."

"I've got a handle on things." She waved her hands, shooing him away in a much gentler but no less insistent way than she had the crane. She tugged her shirt into place, squared her shoulders and aimed herself toward her aunt's house. "Now I need to go take care of my daughter and aunt, thank you."

He waited until she actually raised her foot to march off in a show of self-assured satisfaction before he casually scratched under his chin, looked in the direction of the road leading to the highway and asked, "You mean the aunt and daughter who went off with Claire at least fifteen minutes ago?"

"What? Claire? I didn't hear the car . . . Ugh, I couldn't hear anything but grass and water and bugs and thunder and wind . . . Did you say *fifteen* minutes ago?" She rushed down the road toward the house, paused then pivoted and came back to his side. "Why wasn't that the first thing out of your mouth?"

"Why would it be? I thought you had a handle on things around here," he said plainly, not even a hint of taunting. It only took a couple of steps for him to reach the passenger door of the truck. He swung it open. "Hop in. I'll give you a lift to the house."

"House nothing." Just that quickly she seemed to rebound from her confusion and conflict and he caught a glimpse of the old impulsive Emma layered with a new confidence and certainty. "We're going to go after them."

For so long he had dismissed her readiness to go after what she wanted as flightiness, fear of commitment. But right now, seeing the focus she put into her quick decision making mixed with the fierceness of a mama needing to protect her cub, Hank saw Emma in a whole new light. He couldn't help showing some of that newfound respect as he slid behind the wheel and started the engine. "Yes, ma'am."

He guided the truck onto the drive that went around the house and joined with the old road, seeming to hit every rut, rise and rock.

Emma didn't even appear to notice. When the tires took a dip that rattled the whole vehicle, she just asked, "Can't this thing go faster?"

"Not and stay in one piece it can't." He

took a curve with care. "If you wanted fast you should have let me take you to the house and grabbed your own ride."

"It would have taken too long to get there, find my purse, keys, get moving." She leaned forward, as if those few inches would get her to her daughter all the sooner.

"You act like this is some kind of an emergency. She hasn't been kidnapped. She's with your sister and the woman who raised you."

"Exactly the reason I'm panicky." She shot him a look that he took to say she was only partly kidding. "Aunt Sammie never thinks before doing something like this. It just occurs to her that it might be a teaching moment . . . an opportunity for personal growth or . . . or . . . or just a hoot and a half worth of fun and off she goes."

"But Ruth's not just with Sammie Jo. Claire is with them."

"Claire? Aka Miss I Am In Charge of Everything, Do It All Without Help From Anyone and Think I Know What's Best for Everybody Else, Too?"

"Aka?" He laughed, first at the idea of responsible Claire Newberry being also known as anything. Then at the sibling rivalry between the sisters who were actually very much alike — bold, bright, independent, full of life and faith and mule-headed determination to do what they thought was right even if they had to barrel over a few poor folks who got in their way. He focused, wisely, on the aka thing. "Hmm, I'd have thought Claire, with her penchant for local government work, would have operated under a catchier alias."

"You're probably right about that. Nothing I do ever equals what Claire can do." Resignation, not anger, tempered her voice to a distant murmur. She sighed and shook her head, her gaze forward. "Between her and Sammie Jo they both think they know better about how to raise Ruth. That's one reason why I've never come back to Gall Rive with Ruth."

"One reason?" Yeah, he picked up on that and couldn't resist the question, especially when any other questions were veritable minefields for a man who was still impossibly clinging to his conviction to not get involved.

She didn't look at him, just fixed her eyes on the end of the back road and the beginning of the narrow old highway that lay ahead. "This truck *can* pick up some speed on the good road, right? Who knows where they've gotten to by now."

"Who knows where? You have been away

from Gall Rive too long if you think they can get lost in that town." Up ahead the last of the ominous clouds had begun to dissipate. The sun seemed brighter in contrast. It suited Hank's mood. "Oh, it's true, we do have *three* stoplights now."

"Three? That's like one for every block." She rolled her eyes. "Probably Claire's doing, right?"

"The new owner of the café set up for wireless internet last month, but still serves coffee that looks and tastes like something from the dark ages." He wasn't touching any topic that led back to the sister thing. "Lot of empty storefronts on Main Street these days. Some of them have had occupants come and go, some have signage left over from when Nixon was president. But we have the same half a dozen churches scattered over the town proper and surrounding area. And we have one doctor who runs an actual medical practice now."

"That's one more than we had when I graduated with my BSN and we were . . ."

He could feel her eyes on him. He wanted to look at her, wanted to see if her expression was one of pain or anger, or perhaps even regret. But he had to merge the truck onto the old highway. The quiet stretch of road went for hours without a lone car traveling over it. Of course now it suddenly had a semi and a couple of motorcycles.

"I mean, that's one more doctor in town than when I was deciding whether I wanted to stay in Gall Rive," she concluded.

"Well, this medical thing is a new deal." He decided not to add "put together by Claire." He eased the truck onto the road and headed toward town. "The doc is only there on Tuesdays and Fridays."

"Really?" She tapped her crooked knuckle against her full, pursed lips.

Could this new development actually change how she thought about her old hometown? She'd left because of him, but even if the two of them had gotten married without a doctor or clinic in town, she would have wanted to get out of Gall Rive eventually in order to do the work she felt called to do as a nurse. Not that it mattered to Hank, but as a good citizen of the place he felt obligated to do his part for the community. "Oh, and we have a newly renovated art and cultural center/town museum/library/city hall building now. That also doubles as an after-school child-care center during the school year."

"That's nice."

"Especially for people with school-age kids."

If she got his drift, his small way of letting her know that Gall Rive might not be such a dead-end place for someone like her or too isolated for a child like Ruth, she didn't let on. She just craned her neck and narrowed her eyes, scanning the horizon even though they were still more than three miles from town.

"Anyway, Sammie Jo and Claire are slick characters, I'll grant you that, but I don't suppose even they could hide out for long in Gall Rive." He glanced over at the sign advertising The Good Neighbor Grocery Store that hadn't been updated in a decade. "If we don't spot them a few minutes after we roll into town, I guarantee somebody else will have."

"And they'll be all too happy to get themselves involved in my family's business," she muttered, exasperated but not as snippy as he'd expected she might be under the circumstances.

"I would have said they'd be all too happy to help," he offered, in nearly the same quietly persuasive voice he'd use to get an animal to come to his side.

This time when she looked at him, he stole a glance her way. Their eyes met. She seemed . . . skeptical but open to his view

of the town that was now just on the horizon.

"I just . . . I want to find Ruthie, okay?"
she said softly.

"She's fine, you know." Hank had no
doubt of that. "Your aunt and sister —"

"Are not me." She cut him off to supply
her own ending to that sentence. "They are
not me. I have had to take care of, watch
over, provide for and protect Ruthie her
whole life. Not them. They don't know."

He came to the first stoplight in town. To
their left was the small redbrick building
that housed the new doctor's office. On the
right and down into the next block, the new
multipurpose city hall and community
center. Being a Saturday, this end of town
was pretty much vacant. No one here would
care if they had to wait through a green light
to get an answer to the question he had to
ask the woman he had once hoped to share
his life with. "They don't know what, Em?"

At first she pressed her lips together. She
stared straight ahead.

The light turned green.

Hank did not lift his foot from the brake.

She drew in a long, slow breath and as
she let it out, her voice went watery and her
eyes moist. "They don't know how hard it
can be. How much vigilance it takes to care

for a child like Ruth. They don't understand how the smallest thing can be impossible for her or that just because she wants to do something doesn't mean you should let her try."

The sound of a car coming up behind made Hank check the rearview mirror. Without hesitating and giving her a chance to clam up again, he rolled down his window and motioned the car to go around his truck.

Emma didn't seem to notice. "She's fragile in so many ways. And perpetually frustrated. The world is a difficult and scary place for her. She may never be able to do everything it asks of her on her own."

"You still talking about Ruth or have you started telling me about yourself?"

She lifted her head and met his steady gaze. She sniffled once then again, putting the back of her hand to her nose to try to stifle the side effect of her tears.

He reached behind the seat and grabbed the roll of paper towels he kept back there, usually for cleaning up after veterinary calls, and offered it to her. "It's not a gentleman's fancy white hankie, but . . ."

"Thanks." She unceremoniously tore off a couple of sheets and blew her nose, loud. When she looked up at him, she gave him a meek smile and laugh that told him her moment of vulnerability had passed. "Anyway, Aunt Sammie and Claire are great, don't get me wrong. But they don't do things regarding Ruth the way I want things done. I wouldn't even have left Ruth in Aunt Sammie's care this morning if I hadn't been going down to the pond to deal with that crane. I mean, I couldn't exactly take her along for that, could I?"

"Why not?" The light turned green again and he eased on the gas to set the truck rolling down the street again. "I mean, other than not wanting your daughter to see your less-than-convincing flying-crane imitation."

That managed to get her laughing at herself. She blew her nose again and relaxed against the back of the seat a bit. "It's a pond. She can't swim and doesn't understand about water safety. And I told you about her sudden obsession with that crane. Cranes bite, you said so yourself."

"Are you going to hold *that* over my head the rest of our lives?" Not that there will be a *rest of our lives,* he kept himself from adding. He wasn't the kind to second-guess or qualify every innocent remark. They cruised to the next stoplight. The bank. The barbershop, a florist, the coffee shop/café. No sign of Claire's distinctive baby-blue reconditioned vintage police cruiser. "Look, I hear what you're saying about Ruth, I really do. In my line of work —"

"Uh-uh. No, no, no." She held up her hand to stop him right there. "I know you are not exactly kid friendly, and maybe because of your ideas about children and raising them that you aren't exactly . . . all mushy-gushy when it comes to talking about them but you are *not* going to sit there and try to compare animal training to raising my child, Hank Corsaut."

"Actually, I wasn't." He leaned forward to peer down the side street to make sure they didn't miss Claire and company heading back to the house some other way. "I was going to say that in my line of work I deal with *people* training as much or more than animal training. My opinion? A lot of what you're worried about is well within your ability to control, to change and/or make better."

A little of the starch came back into her posture. "So, once again, *I'm* the problem?"

"Did I say you were the problem?" As the truck rolled slowly forward he swept his gaze over the end of the street, where the town's lone grocery store stood across the way from a hardware, used junk, fix-it shop sporting a gold-and-black sign reading Leverett's All Goods that Gall Rive residents had come, in the last few years, to call simply by the owner's nickname — Ray Bob's. If they weren't at the doctor's then these were the most likely places to find the trio. No baby-blue police car in sight. "We didn't get married all those years ago because I am the kind of man who says what he means, and means what he says. *That* much hasn't changed. If I thought you were the problem, I'd have said so."

She gripped the door handle and looked at him, her lips pressed into a thin line. He didn't know if she wanted to thank him for that or bite his head off for bringing up their past.

"As for not being mushy-gushy about kids? Yeah, that hasn't changed, either, but then from what little time I spent with that kid of yours, Em, mushy-gushy isn't going to do her any favors." He shook his head and trained his gaze on Emma again. "What Ruth needs is —"

"Hank! Look out!" Emma screamed. Her hand shot out toward the windshield. "Stop! Stop!"

Hank turned his head just in time to see a small blond blur running into the street in front of his truck.

CHAPTER FIVE

Emma braced herself for the sickening screech of tires.

That did not happen.

In reality, Hank's truck had barely been moving and with Ruth in the street a good two car lengths away from them, he brought the vehicle to a shuddering stop with just a light tap on the brakes. The whole thing took maybe three seconds.

In less time than that, Emma had scrambled out of the seat and into the wide, empty street. Her feet pounded over the pavement to close the distance between the front bumper of Hank's old truck and the spot where her aunt was, even now, grabbing her excited child by the hand to hold her in place.

Claire got to them the same time Emma did.

Ruthie squirmed and stretched and reached from her tippy toes to her fingertips to try to get herself even an inch closer to whatever had drawn her into the street in the first place. The child let out a squeal of utter, exasperated, futile frustration.

Emma knew exactly how her daughter felt.

"First you cart my daughter off without even asking me." She pressed her hand to her chest and struggled to get a good full breath. The humid Louisiana summer air taxed her lungs as the dank mingling of moss and mold and fresh-cut grass from the nearby houses burned her sinuses. Her head throbbed. Adrenaline made her knees weak and gave her words a hard, harsh edge. "Then you don't even watch her while she's in your care?"

"Emma, this is a prime example of what I tried to tell you about people and their ability to control and change behaviors." The sound of Hank's door slamming as he got out of his truck wrenched her attention — and her ire — in his direction.

"And *you!*" She blinked back the tears as she shouted at the man she had just begun to trust again, the man she had almost poured her heart out to, almost let her guard down with for the first time in too many years to count. She could feel the actual sensation of bitterness swelling into the back of her throat. "Don't you talk to me about people and change. You don't know anything about me anymore, much less about my daughter and my life."

She reached for Ruth's hand.

The child evaded her grasp.

Sammie Jo and Claire simply stood there, a little bit stunned, a little bit peeved and a whole lot of useless in wrangling the small-for-her-age eight-year-old, Ruth.

"I can't count on anyone else." Emma choked back the threatening tears as she spoke more to drive the point home to herself than for the people around her. She fought back against duel sucker punches of fear and pain she felt all too often when trying to figure out how to be the kind of parent Ruth needed her to be. "Taking care of Ruth is my responsibility and mine alone. I can see that now."

"Oh, honey, that's just the fret talking. No use getting all worked up over this. It's over now and everything is all right." Sammie Jo kept her hold on Ruth with one hand and used the other to propel the little girl toward the other side of the street. "After all it was just a little harmless jaywalking."

"Jay . . . ?" Emma glanced back at Hank to see if he had heard the wild understatement.

He smiled. Actually smiled. He was still

smiling when he got back into his truck and parked it behind Claire's car in front of the Good Neighbor Grocery Store.

If Emma had been a different kind of person and she'd have had one handy, she believed she might have thrown a rock at the man's crummy old truck just to show him what she thought of his attitude about it all.

"Oh, Emma, please. It's Gall Rive." Claire gave a dismissive wave of her hand and a toss of her head, sending her hair flipping over the shoulder of her perfectly fitted summer sundress. "There wasn't a car in sight until Hank's truck up and started rolling our way. If you hadn't come barreling full tilt out of that truck right at her, the girl would have been safely on the other side of the street by the time he got down to this part of town."

On one hand, she couldn't argue with the facts or with Claire, who had laid them out so plainly. On the other hand she had just had her child taken without permission and ended up finding that child darting across a street half a block away from the crosswalk.

"And for the record?" Claire looked over her shoulder and nailed her sister with a cool, accomplished look. "We were never more than two steps behind her."

Emma watched them walk away, her mouth hanging open. When she found the power to speak she reminded them, "She was in the street. My child was in the middle of the street!"

"Shouts the woman standing in the middle of that same street to the child now safe and sound on the sidewalk where she belongs." Hank pressed his hand to the taut muscles between her shoulder blades to nudge her along. "Children learn by example, let's be a good one."

There wasn't a condescending or judgmental note in a single word of what he had said, which only made Emma all the more irritated with him. If he had gone all snotty and I-know-how-to-deal-with-Ruth-better-than-you-do on her she'd have felt justified in striking out at him, or at least jerking away from him and flouncing off on her own. As it was she let the air out of her lungs slowly, nodded her agreement and walked side by side with Hank, trying not to give in to the welcome and familiar comfort she found in the warmth of his touch.

Just as she forced herself not to dwell on how alone and let down she felt the instant his hand dropped away. They stepped up onto the sidewalk where she found herself standing in the shadow of Ray Bob's storefront with her aunt and sister as they indulged Ruth's admiring a row of shiny bicycles.

"Pretty!" Ruth patted the sparkling banana seat of a turquoise vintage Sting-Ray bicycle.

"I swan, Ray Bob, all these pretty bikes with their fancy dodads and geegaws. I do believe you have created what they call in the insurance business a 'beautiful nuisance.' "

"Good morning, lovely ladies. And I believe the term you mean, my dear, is 'attractive nuisance' in that it is not only lovely to the eye but beguiles people to approach despite the potential danger." Ray Bob lifted Sammie Jo's hand in his and bent over it, clearly intent on kissing it. But before he did, he glanced up and added, "May I say, it's a term I might personally apply to you, Miss Samantha Jolene Newberry."

"Why, Ray Bob, I have to watch you every minute, the way you talk." Sammie Jo demurred like a thoroughly enamored young woman. She flipped her hand over and gave his cheek a pat. "You do say the sweetest things."

"More!" Ruth moved on to the next bike, squatting down to ooh and aah over the plastic beads attached to the spokes of the wheels.

Emma leaned back to whisper to Hank out of the corner of her mouth, "That was *sweet?*"

"You have been away too long if you've forgotten how these two flirt with each other," he muttered back.

Ray Bob Leverett and Sammie Jo Newberry could have been one of the great love stories of their time. High-school sweethearts separated when Ray Bob's father insisted his son go to a distant college to earn a degree in business. They had always held a fondness for one another that had just begun to rekindle when Claire and Emma's parents were killed and suddenly Sammie Jo had to turn her attention to raising the girls and keeping a roof over their heads.

After years of waiting for Sammie Jo to agree to marry him, Ray Bob moved to another state and married another woman. After his wife died, he had moved back into town to take over the struggling family business. It had taken pretty much all his time and a considerable amount of his life savings, but he had kept the doors to the old place open.

Sammie Jo had relayed all these details in what she called the "newsy little notes from home" portion of her emails. What those notes had not revealed was just how much her aunt still cared for her first love — and that he clearly felt the same.

Emma pressed her fingertips against her temples and willed herself not to make comparisons between Sammie Jo and Ray Bob's story and her and Hank's. They weren't the same. Those two had been torn apart by circumstances and the desire to do the right thing for others, not by the single-minded selfishness of one of the parties involved. They had put family and home first, whereas Hank had completely shut out even the possibility of their having a family together. Not the same at all. She took a deep breath and only then realized how much her heart was aching over all of this. She blinked and a tear clung to her eyelash.

Ruth found a red boy's bike with an old-fashioned bell on the handlebar. She gave it a squeeze. It chirped out a *br-r-ring-br-r-ring* and she laughed.

Emma sniffled and forced herself to speak calmly, even a bit curtly as she tipped her head toward Hank, standing behind her, again and said, "I was pretty young the last time I saw Aunt Sammie and Ray Bob together. I don't remember much about it but now that I do see them, it reinforces my conviction that I cannot stay around here one minute longer than absolutely necessary. Sammie Jo deserves her chance at love without her family getting in the way."

"Funny way of putting it. Here I thought families were *about* love." He made an all-inclusive gesture with his hands, creating a circle in the air. When he drew his hands together, he laced his fingers together and tugged to show how difficult it was to break the connection. "The more love around, the stronger all the relationships can be."

His words shook her to the root of her being, not just for the truth of them but for the way they applied to the personal conflict that had brought her back to Gall Rive, back to this spot, standing here beside this man. That Hank, of all people, was saying this tied her emotions into knots. Had he really changed so much? Or was he just parroting what he thought she believed? She tried to find the answers in his eyes but before she could see or say anything Ruth's voice rang out.

"Mine! This one is for me. It's pink, pink, pink!" She threw her arms out to encompass a child-size bike from the pink plastic basket in front to the pink and white seat sitting atop a pink glittered frame. Laying one cheek against the pink-and-white-tasseled pom-pom cascading from the white rubber handgrip, she sighed then raised her excitement-filled eyes to Emma and asked, "What is it?"

Claire, Ray Bob and Sammie Jo burst out laughing in clear delight at Ruth's ability to be so sure she loved something even when she didn't know what it was.

"I wish every customer came by this old place had your enthusiasm for the merchandise, darlin'." Ray Bob clapped his meaty hands together.

"You mean to tell me this kid has never seen a bicycle?" Claire cut straight to the chase, her arms folded and her eyes shooting accusations of bad parenting Emma's way.

"She's seen cyclists in the city plenty of times," Emma snapped. "But, I don't guess she's ever seen a child's bike. Not up close, maybe not at all. It's not like children are allowed to ride them up and down the hallways of our apartment building. Or like she would ever be able to ride one her . . ."

"This is a bicycle, kiddo." Hank stepped forward and caught Ruth under each arm.

". . . self." Emma stepped forward, her hand raised to stop him. One of Ruth's issues was sensory response. She didn't like to be touched and liked even less being in

102

any way restrained. "What are you doing, Hank? Please. You'll upset her."

Ruth didn't so much as grunt or wriggle in protest at Hank intervening.

He deftly lifted the petite child up and settled her on the seat.

Emma tried to get in close to make sure the bike didn't fall over but Claire edged in ahead of her, gripping the handlebar and back fender to add some stability.

Sammie Jo and Ray Bob shuffled in closer, too, leaning one way then the other to get a better view of the event.

Emma looked at all of them, unable to believe they were just rushing in and taking over parenting duties for *her* child. A moment ago she had complained that she had sole responsibility for her child; now she *wished* that were the case. She wanted to push these interlopers aside, to take charge, to tell them all they didn't know what they were doing. They didn't recognize Ruth's limitations or understand how they were setting her up for a physical fall or an emotional crash, or both.

Hank pressed his knees against the seat to make sure the kickstand wasn't the only thing keeping the bike upright. "You put your feet on those pedals down there and push to make it move. When you get the

103

knack of it, you just hop on and go, go, go."

"I can go?" Ruth could hardly sit still on the seat. Her feet kicked at the pedals without ever settling onto them properly. "I can go fast?"

"As fast as your little legs can pedal." Claire bent down low, cheek to cheek with Ruth. "It's like flying, baby girl."

"I can fly! Mommy, I can fly!" Ruth's legs went swinging, she bent low over the handlebars, never so much as glancing back at Emma.

Even though the bicycle didn't budge an inch, Emma's stomach lurched as if she had just experienced a free fall in a plummeting elevator. *Fly? Ruth?*

First her family had carted her child off without asking. Now they were putting ideas in her head about flying away . . . from home . . . from Emma . . . on her own . . . alone.

"This is not what I came here for!" The words came out of Emma like a bottle rocket streaking across a star-strewn sky.

And she got about the same reaction from the group as she would have if she had set off a firework right there on the sidewalk.

"Emma, we're just trying to —" Hank didn't get a chance to finish before Claire chimed in.

"What's the matter with you?" Claire's eyes went all squinty.

"I'm sorry. I hope you don't think I was pushing for you to buy the bike, Emma." Ray Bob looked genuinely remorseful for his part in it all. "Your girl was just so happy about it. It seemed a shame for her not to get to test drive her dream, if only for a moment."

His words stunned her. Ruth, happy. Those were terms she didn't often hear. Not that Ruth was an angry child or despondent. In fact, most of the time she was just . . . Ruth. A little sweet, a little funny, a little curious, a little strange, a little distant, a little too stubborn to be trusted to obey rules that most people took for granted. "What a lovely idea, Ray Bob, that Ruthie could try out a dream. But I'm afraid —"

"Say no more." Sammie Jo spread her arms out, her hands open. She started for the door of the store like a majorette leading a marching band out to take the field. "We didn't come here for a bicycle, Ray Bob, honey. We came for a few necessities."

He held his hand out to the door of his establishment. "I'll venture I have whatever you want."

"And a few things I didn't even know I wanted yet," Sammie Jo said with a coquettish tilt of her head that made yet another pair of handmade earrings flash in the sunlight. Still, they hardly matched the twinkle in Sammie Jo's eyes when she winked at her old beau. "But let's start with the basics. Sidewalk chalk? Big bottle of bubble liquid?"

"Got it. Got it." Ray Bob nodded.

Ruth's feet kept clunking against the pedals, now in a steady *thumpity-thump* rhythm with much less urgency than before. "Go. Pink. Fly away, fly."

"A water sprinkler. A dozen Mason jars. Long-handled tweezers." As Sammie Jo spoke she ticked each item off on her fingers. "A big plastic tool chest. And an army surplus backpack."

"All that and so much more, right this way." Ray Bob led Sammie Jo inside.

"That should be enough for a start." Sammie Jo disappeared behind him. "You know, just a few of the usual things a kid needs to keep from being bored on a long summer day."

Hank folded his arms and shook his head as Sammie Jo and Ray Bob headed into the store. "I get the bubbles and chalk, but tweezers? Toolbox? Army surplus?"

"She just wants to provide Ruthie with the same kind of amazing summers that

Emma and I had out at the bird sanctuary."
Claire ran her fingers through Ruth's fine
blond hair. She took a step back, at last,
from the bike.

Emma pushed her way in to take Claire's
place, immediately grabbing the handlebars
and the back of the seat to keep Ruth secure.

"Running through a water sprinkler, col-
lecting treasures in a tool chest, racing over
the lawn at dusk with an open Mason jar to
gather up enough lightning bugs to make a
lantern." Claire made a graceful motion
with her hand as though she had that jar
and was running through a field scooping
up clusters of glowing bugs. "Simple things
that give a child the kind of memories she
can't get from a video game or the TV set."

To hear Claire describe it, Emma suddenly not only longed to provide the same
experiences for Ruth, she also sort of wished
she could relive them herself.

Ruth's foot knocked vainly against the
pedal again hard, then harder. She gritted
her teeth and leaned even lower on the bike,
her feet flailing faster. "Go! Pink! Fly!"

But Emma had long ago outgrown the
simple childhood things of summers past.

"Ruth, kicking the bike is not the way to
make it work. You have to be taught how to
ride one and we can't do that here or now."

Hank reached down to remove the small girl.

"No! Go! Fly!" Ruth wailed.

And Ruth was not a simple child. No matter how much people thought that they could say or do or buy the right things to make the child more . . . more "normal" . . . that was not going to happen.

"Y'all never should have interfered," Emma said with resigned control as she moved in and took Ruth from Hank. Holding the child close, in a hold meant to lend comfort but also to prevent flailing, kicking and head banging that might hurt the child, Emma cooed nonspecific assurances to try to keep Ruth calm.

"You call that interfering?" Hank gestured toward the small pink bicycle. "I thought we were —"

"No! Go. Go." Ruth pushed at Emma's shoulder then twisted around to try to reach for the pink bike.

The tighter Emma held the child, the more Ruth rebelled against the technique that Emma had begun to realize she hadn't actually used in a couple of years. Ruth was reverting to old behaviors and dragging Emma back with her.

"We have to get out of here," she muttered under her breath. She started toward the street and found her way barricaded by the row of bicycles. She clenched her teeth. "This is too much. It's overwhelming."

"Overwhelming? Emma, c'mon." Hank rubbed his hand up her arm. He moved out of her way then bent at the knees just enough to put his face close enough to speak to Ruth. "She's a kid having a temper tantrum."

"Mine. It's my flying," she told him through huffs of breath, then added stubbornly but softly, "Go. Go."

"I hear ya, kiddo." He touched her nose then met Emma's gaze. "More to the point, she's a Newberry woman pitching a bona fide hissy fit. Don't make more of it than it deserves."

"Don't you make this about me," she snapped. She wrenched away and Ruth's shoe hit the handle of the first of the row of bicycles. The whole row went cascading down like dominoes.

Ruth grunted.

Claire groaned and rolled her eyes even as she began to right the bikes one at a time.

Emma let her sister take care of it. "You don't have any right to comment on this, Hank. This doesn't involve you."

"Oh, hey!" He backed off, both hands held up. "The last thing I am is involved. I just wanted —"

Emma moved to the right and Hank was in front of her. To the left, and he had moved there, not to block her, but in his attempt to get out of her way.

Bam-bam-bam. Sammie Jo rapped on the store window and held up a butterfly net for Emma's approval.

"She's so excited to have y'all here, Em." Claire set the last bike, the pretty pink one, upright again, then cocked one hip and stared at Emma with her toned, tanned arms laced over her floral-and-lace bodice. "I'm with Hank. Don't throw it all away because your kid is being a kid."

Emma pulled her back up straight, determined not to acknowledge the man her sister was siding with with so much as a look.

Ruth squealed. Her face went red and sweat beaded on her forehead.

"It's a wonderful thought, Claire, but not realistic." Emma had outgrown childhood joys and she had to face the fact that Ruth might never move past her childish impulses. No one else understood the way she did. People thought they knew what they were dealing with, but dealing with Ruth's issues was a lifelong commitment, not a wistful summer's whim. Emma ducked her head to cut off eye contact with Claire and Sammie Jo, too. She edged her way around the protruding bicycles like a person navigating the narrow ledge outside a ten-story high-rise. "We're not going to be here long enough to need any of that stuff. Go in there and put a stop to all this, please, Claire."

"You're the one being unrealistic. You want to break Aunt Sammie's heart?" Claire did not budge. "You have to do it yourself."

"Have you forgotten? You're the sister who gets things done." Emma snuggled Ruth's hot face close but managed to look at Claire with one eye. "I'm the sister who runs away."

"So if I go in there and deal with this what are you going to do?"

She cupped Ruth's head as the child finally grew quieter. "I'm going to have Hank take Ruth and me back to the house."

"Oh, really? That's your plan?" Claire shook her head and headed for the open door of the old store. Just before she went inside she leaned out and tipped her head toward the street and added, "Well, then, you'd better run because Hank is driving away right now."

CHAPTER SIX

"He did *not* leave you stranded." Claire held the door to Ray Bob's open for Emma and Ruth. "I have a car and I had planned to take Aunt Sammie and Ruth back to the sanctuary anyway. If you ask me nice, I'll probably let you ride along."

For a split second Emma was torn between easing the tension by taking her ribbing with a smile and the natural inclination to stick her tongue out and stamp past in classic bratty-little-sister style. She chose to accept the offer with a murmured "thanks" as she swept Ruth across the threshold.

The cool air hit them face first like a blast from a deep freeze flung suddenly open. Emma tipped back her head and reveled in it.

Ruth did the same, and Claire, as well.

It was only then that Emma realized she'd been sweating and uncomfortable in her borrowed clothes and the unaccustomed climate. Atlanta wasn't much farther north than Gall Rive but it had an entirely different kind of heat. Here the air felt heavier. As if it sank into a person. The sun and earth, sky and water, God and His creation all connected for her in this place.

Here Emma had a sense of being enveloped by her surroundings. She wouldn't go so far as to say it made her feel as though she belonged, but the familiarity of it did give rise to an emotional openness she never felt in the city.

She could not entirely shrug off that perception as she walked into Leverett's All Goods Store, a place where she had spent many a Saturday afternoon as a child, where she had bought the very suitcase she took with her when she left Gall Rive — when she left Hank Corsaut — so many years ago. Things had sure come full circle, she thought, as she stood there still stinging over Hank taking off without an explanation a few minutes earlier.

She ushered Ruth into the large open space. The child craned her neck to try to take in the wall-to-wall collection of just *stuff.* Tools and toys, garden implements and gym clothes. Rebuilt lawn mowers and little rubber rowboats. Ray Bob had stocked his store with all of that and so much more.

"Now if you don't want the expense of something new, I probably could find you a used one in the back of the store. Might need a touch of paint . . . require a little elbow grease to get the rust scraped off . . . and some engineering savvy to figure out how to get the wheels all aimed in the same direction . . ." Ray Bob towered above the floor on a ladder against the far wall, lugging down a large box with the picture of a wood-sided little red wagon on the front. "But I can let you have it for a song."

"What song would that be, Ray Bob, darling?" Sammie Jo sang out an old children's rhyme she'd taught the girls when they were young as she hovered around the bottom rungs with her hands up as if that would insure he didn't drop his cargo. When she noticed Emma out of the corner of her eye she had the decency to look at least a little guilty. "I know. *I know!* It's too much."

"Too-oo much," Ruth parroted one of her own favorite phrases in Aunt Sammie's Louisiana cadence.

"But I saw it up there and . . . of course it looks to you like I'm going totally overboard but I was gonna need me one of these anyway," Sammie Jo justified. "And after all, this *is* Ruthie's first summer with us at the sanctuary."

Emma ground her back teeth together to keep from making a comment she might later regret. She didn't intend to stick around all summer but Sammie Jo wasn't in any frame of mind to listen to that nor would Emma's saying it have any effect on this wild buying spree, which had Sammie Jo lit up like a Gall Rive Bay fishing boat decked out stem to stern with decorations at Christmas.

"What do you think, pretty-great kid of mine?" Sammie Jo held both arms open wide to invite her pretty-great niece to join her in her summer of spoiling Ruth shoppingfest. "You want a wagon?"

Emma raised her chin to call out to caution her aunt not to be too extravagant and not to get her expectations up regarding things like Ruth rushing into a hug much less participating in planned activities.

"I want a wagon!" Ruth did her version of skipping, which looked a bit like barely controlled tripping, right off to Sammie Jo. "What else do I want, Great-aunt Sammie? Show me!"

"A girl after my own heart if ever there was one," Sammie Jo gushed as she held her hand out to Ruth and left poor Ray Bob to deal with the boxed wagon on his own.

"I tell ya I am not as young as I used to be." Ray Bob lowered himself down slowly, settled the box on the floor then made a big show of rubbing his lower back and letting out a long, dramatic groan. "If you can, do ole Ray Bob a big favor, little lady, and have your Great-aunt Sammie want things for you that aren't so high up out of reach."

"We'll see. But a girl wants what a girl wants. You know that, Ray Bob, sugar. Ruth and I will try to be good stewards of your back and her mother's patience, though." Aunt Sammie did have the consideration to glance at Emma for a kind of permission, and to send a wink her way that made clear the older woman would probably do just as she pleased anyway. "C'mon, sweetie, let's have us a good look around."

Emma gave her aunt a weak nod to proceed. Not even a full day in Gall Rive, and she'd already begun to lose control. It should have troubled her more. It did trouble her; she was just a bit amazed that it didn't bother her *more*. Probably just because she was tired and in an emotional muddle.

Sammie Jo paused in the aisle long enough to pluck a hot-pink sun hat off a tall rack. She plopped it on Ruth's head.

Emma braced herself for a hat-throwing,

hair-pulling temper fit.

Ruth put both hands on the hat brim and grinned. "I want this?"

"It's you!"

"I'm me!" Ruth squealed and ran off, still clutching the hat brim.

Emma tugged at the cotton shirt clinging to her back, wishing she could capture a few ounces of that kind of enthusiasm for just being herself. Exasperated at just about everything, she finally turned to Claire as if their conversation about Hank had hardly skipped a beat. "All I'm saying is Hank brought me into town. He stuck his nose into my business by putting Ruth on that bike. Then for him to just up and disappear without so much as a goodbye, leaving me and my child to fend for ourselves? What kind of a man does that?"

"A better kind of man than I think you are giving him credit for being, Em. A better man than you *ever* credited him for being." Claire tipped her head toward the man now framed by the large picture window overlooking Main Street in the front of the musty, cluttered store.

"Oh, so he came back after being a thoughtless jerk and that makes him a hero?" She copped that attitude as much because of her crossness with her sister's defense of Hank as for the nerve of the man himself, leaving her high and dry and then waltzing back in as if nothing had happened.

He raised his hand to wave to someone down the street. A passing car slowed, the passenger rolled down the window and shouted something to him. He moved from greeting to a thumbs-up.

All right, she thought, he wasn't exactly waltzing.

Striding would better describe his long-legged, determined gait. Each footfall set his thick, dark hair sweeping over his shirt collar or shifting forward until enough fell forward to brush over his eyes. He swiped it back in one surprisingly liquid motion with his large hand while he held a box of some kind under his other arm. The hair did not stay put and when it grazed the resolute creases in his forehead a second time, he gave his head a toss to flick it back into place.

He reached for the door handle and when two older ladies came walking arm in arm up the sidewalk, he held it open for them. They cooed and fussed over him and gave him little girlish waves. He held the door, waiting for them to get to it. The late-morning sun streaked across his back and highlighted the width and strength of his broad shoulders.

He had been young when they had dated, but not a kid. He'd already been through college and vet school, after all. Still, she remembered him being a little on the skinny side with an eagerness to fit into life in Gall Rive that he wore like a new military recruit might wear an oversize hat or boots that had not quite gotten broken in yet.

"You are just the dearest thing, Dr. Corsaut." One of the dark-skinned women, her words an amicable blend of age and accent, gave his arm a pat as they passed by. "I don't know what we'd do without you."

Clearly he no longer needed to work at fitting in.

"Dr. Corsaut took such good care of my Mr. Pickles last year," the other woman said, her nose tipped up a bit as if just having her pet cared for by Hank constituted an elevated social status.

"And he teaches Sunday school!" the other woman chimed in.

"Oh, I know! If I had a granddaughter I'd certainly point her in his direction" came the ready agreement from her companion. "Many's the time I've said that a man of his caring nature and powerful personal charm should be married with half a dozen children under his roof."

Hank was part of this place now. As much a part of it as Claire, or Sammie Jo, or Ray Bob's.

Emma didn't even recognize these two ladies. She had missed out on Ray Bob's return and had no idea how much he and Aunt Sammie flirted. She was the outsider now.

"Haven't I told you that, Dr. Corsaut?" Mr. Pickles's owner shook one bony finger in Hank's direction. "Married with six children. At least!"

And Emma wasn't sure how she felt about that.

"Yes, ma'am." He gave the ladies a sincere smile and kind nod. When he raised his gaze to meet Emma's his mouth took on a wry twist on one side as he added, "I'll get to work on that soon as I have a chance."

She wasn't sure how she felt about that at all!

He let the door fall shut, adjusted the box under his arm and headed her way. No doubt about it, he belonged here just as much as she belonged . . . somewhere. Emma ran her hand down her long braid. Wasn't that why she had come running back to Gall Rive, because she wasn't sure where she should spend the rest of her life? Only, the night she had run out of that fancy restaurant, Hank had not even remotely been a part of the equation.

Not that he held any sway over her ultimate decisions. Nor had he indicated he would like to have a say. But seeing him now as the man he had become and having seen him with Ruth as the man he could be, it couldn't help but make Emma wonder about the kind of man she needed in her life, whether as a good friend, a father figure for Ruth or as a husband.

Husband? Had she really allowed herself to let that thought form in her mind while looking directly at the heartwarming and a little bit breath-stopping sight that was Hank Corsaut?

Oh, no, she was not going there, not even a little bit. Emma drew back her shoulders, readied herself for the moment the man came to a stop at her side. Then she'd remind him — and herself — of the not-so-friendly or father-figurely, much less husbandly stunt he had just pulled. "Nice of you to come back for me, Mr. Caring Nature and Powerful Personal Charm."

He looked down, right into her eyes, and cocked his head, saying softly, "That's *Doctor* Caring Nature and Powerful Personal Charm, if you don't mind."

"Right, right. You've got a DVM, I've got a Ph.D., every other person around is a doctor." Claire propped one arm up on Emma's back.

Emma shot her a quick look and rolled her shoulder to shrug off her sister's casual gesture.

"But only one of us took off like his tail was on fire then showed back up carting a box into a store that already has just about everything anyone could possibly need, except . . ." Claire did not hesitate or even ask permission, she just reached out and yanked the box from under Hank's arm. "Yes! I thought that was what I saw peeking out from under there. Look, Em, your troubles with Ruth and the bicycle are solved!"

Still smarting from that "every other person is a doctor" remark from her super-successful sister, it took Emma a moment to pry her gaze off Claire's beaming expression and actually look at what Hank had brought. When she did, she felt punched in the gut. "A helmet? You brought my special-needs child a *helmet?*"

Images of comedians making jokes ridiculing stupid people as needing helmets, of people with disabilities that required they wear helmets daily for their own physical protection filled her head.

"No, I didn't bring a special-needs kid a helmet. I brought Ruth the proper equipment that every kid needs for basic bicycle safety. Or beginner pony riding, which is why I sell these at my clinic." He sank both hands into the open box and whipped out a set of knee and elbow pads. "You get Ray Bob to round you up a set of training wheels and Ruth will be flying on that pink bike before you can say —"

"No!" She stepped backward, unable to believe what she was seeing and hearing. "No. It's not that easy. Don't you understand? Ruth isn't . . . She can't . . . No, no, *you two can't.* And Aunt Sammie can't. You can't override my parenting decisions. I know my child and do what's best for her. Ruth *cannot* ride a bike."

"Then you teach her how to ride one." Hank pitched the pads back into the box in Claire's hands.

"I'm not just saying she doesn't know how to ride, Hank." Despite the supercooled air in the store, a trickle of sweat snaked down Emma's neck. She shivered. "I'm saying she is not able."

"So, you've tried before?" he asked.

"No, but I know my child." Another step away from them both. "I know her life. I have watched her frustration turn to near rage and disintegrate into waves of angry or inconsolable sobbing."

"Oh, Em, honey." Claire swung her hand not holding the box out and snagged Emma by the hand, gave a squeeze then let go.

"But that's not every time, Emma." Hank shifted his boots and the old floor creaked. "Yeah, I've only been around the kid for an afternoon. I don't know her every mood and difficulty. But I do know that she's feisty, she's curious and she's resilient."

"Do you know that every day, I pray for her to just have a good day? Do you know what that's like, Hank?" She swallowed hard to try to quell the quiver in her voice. She paced across the floor and faced the shelf stacked with compasses and camping gear. "I don't pray for her to do anything amazing, though she amazes me all the time. I just pray for her not to get hurt or to be mistreated, laughed at or rejected or to lose hope."

The floor creaked as Claire shifted forward and Emma edged another few steps away.

"Every day something Ruth does makes me laugh." Emma's throat was raw with emotion. Her eyes stung with tears. She stared blankly at the maps and atlases literally at her fingertips. "Every day something she does or someone else does scares me. It's too much to ask me to set her up for more of that, to set her up for failure."

Hank came up behind her so close that she could feel his shirt against her back. He brushed her braid over her shoulder.

She tensed, her shoulders raised as if to create a wall to keep him out.

He crooked one finger and fit it under her chin. Gently, he turned her face to his and asked, "What if she doesn't fail?"

"What if . . ." Emma whispered. Oh, how she wanted to consider that possibility. She really did. But her heart just couldn't risk it, not when Ruth was so vulnerable.

"Oh, I know what else you want, Ruthie-girl," Aunt Sammie's cheerful claim came from just around the corner, out of sight but not out of earshot. "A big watering can so you can plant some seeds and take care of them and watch them grow."

"*I* can grow! Is it pink?"

"Get the ladder, Ray Bob, the pink watering can is up as high as that wagon was."

"It doesn't matter." Emma shut her eyes and pulled away from Hank. "I'm not having this discussion. We won't be sticking around Gall Rive long enough to find out either way. Certainly not long enough to buy a bicycle and take lessons."

"Not sticking around? I thought you were going to pitch in and help Aunt Sammie." Claire set the box down with a clunk. "You're the nurse."

"You say that like it's an accusation," Emma said. Her emotions churning, she pushed past Hank and moved on down the aisle among the camouflage clothing, hunting knives and portable floodlights for immobilizing deer. "I know it's a good thing I got here when I did. Don't you think I see God's hand in that? But I can't stay here indefinitely."

"Aunt Sammie's meds are still a mess. She won't listen to her doctor. Or me." Claire moved along behind Emma, whispering to keep their aunt from overhearing the discussion. "You and Ruth — you mostly because she wants to keep you happy to be able to do more things with Ruth — are our best chance for getting her health issues sorted out."

"I understand that. I want to help, but I have a life. I have . . . or I *had* a job." No telling if she had one now, since she left the doctor she worked for literally in the lurch work-wise and life-wise when she ran out on him at the restaurant. She knew it would be all right for a couple of days, and he'd understand a family emergency, but she was going to have to call him soon. That meant she'd have to give him some kind of answer. Too bad she didn't have one. "I can't stay here indefinitely."

Hank did not follow her this time. He braced the heel of his hand against the shelf and narrowed his eyes at her. "So you're just going to bug out again?"

She whipped around with the kind of energy that comes from feeling hurt and trapped, and asked, much louder than she intended, *"Again?"*

"It's just a watering can, Emma, honey. I was gonna need one of them, too." Sammie Jo didn't wait for a reply to the sugary-sweet rationalization. "Hold the ladder still, Ray Bob. I'm going up."

Emma pressed her lips together, took a second to compose herself, then went back toward Hank and Claire, speaking barely above a whisper to keep her Aunt Sammie from thinking she was scolding her. "I did not bug out on you, Hank. You hit me with a totally unacceptable stipulation on our relationship. I loved you but I knew even then I wanted to work as a nurse, which I could not have done then in Gall Rive, and I wanted children."

Hank did not deny what she had said or try to apologize for his actions then or his

127

words now.

Emma took a deep breath and with the scent of rust and dust and Louisiana summer air swirling in her head and the old hurt and memories weighing down her heart she whispered hoarsely, "I just followed my dreams."

Hank cocked his head toward her. "Then why don't you let Ruth do the same?"

That was a good question. So good a question that just hearing it made Emma want to burst into tears, not because she didn't have an answer, but because she didn't have an answer she wanted to say out loud.

"I know it scares you but at some point you are going to have to let go of Ruth a little." There was a gentleness about Hank that he had not had in his younger days, an openness and empathy that he wore as easily as he claimed his place in the community. "Better to use every day you have with her to teach her how to be as independent and strong as the woman who is raising her, as strong as —"

"Samantha Jolene?" Concern was instantly evident in Ray Bob's voice. "You okay?"

Thumping and scuffling followed by a crash sent a chill up Emma's spine. Before another word was spoken Emma was on the move.

"Claire . . . someone . . . come quick," Ray Bob called out loud enough to reach the farthest corners of the large, rambling building. "Sammie needs your help."

"I'm here," Emma called out over her thundering footsteps. "Don't worry, Aunt Sammie, I'm here."

CHAPTER SEVEN

"I'm a nurse." Emma pushed past the two women who had come in before Hank and knelt on the floor beside her aunt. She checked for head bumps or gashes first then held Aunt Sammie's face in both hands and looked at her pupils. "What happened?"

"It's no big deal." Aunt Sammie wrapped her tanned and freckled hand around Emma's pale wrist, meant to offer comfort, no doubt. "I was climbing down the ladder, missed a couple rungs and lost my grip on the watering can."

"It *is* a big deal." The hem of Claire's flouncy sundress bounced up and down slightly as she tapped her foot to make sure everyone around could see her vexation with the woman who had raised her. "Whether you want to accept it or not, high blood pressure is a serious health issue, Aunt Sammie."

In the guise of helping her aunt move from

half leaning against the off-kilter ladder to a more comfy position, Emma felt along her arms and back, watching carefully for any signs of tenderness. "Have you been taking your meds, Aunt Sammie?"

"As directed." The older woman yanked her arm away and sat up, looking fine, if a bit pale. "Now will y'all stop treating me like I had another one of those tacky tachycardia episodes? I just slipped a bit. Why all the fuss?"

Ray Bob righted the ladder and rested it a few feet away from the huddled group. "You could have hurt yourself, Samantha Jolene."

"Or someone else," Emma rushed to say before Sammie Jo could launch a protest. Emma shifted her gaze pointedly to Ruth, who stood nearby hugging the dented pink watering can, her straw hat knocked to the floor, her eyes wide. It wasn't that Emma was actually worried about Ruth in this case, but she knew her aunt's biggest weakness and she was not one bit ashamed to use it to drive home the point that Sammie Jo had to take better care of herself.

"I never thought about that." Sammie Jo's slender shoulders slumped forward slightly.

Emma slid her fingers along her aunt's callused hand until they rested on the pulse point of her inner wrist. She wasn't planning on counting the beats per second but did need to see if it was abnormally slow or fast. "So tell me what happened before you missed the ladder rungs. Any dizziness?"

"Dizzy seems a bit extreme. Let's say woozy. I felt a wee bit woozy."

Emma shook her head. She looked up thinking she'd find Claire standing over them and the two sisters would share an eye-rolling moment that only daughters of an impossibly stubborn mother could appreciate. Instead her eyes met Hank's. She instantly lost track of her aunt's pulse rate but became oddly aware of her own heartbeat and how those dark, kind eyes fixing on her made it race harder and faster.

"How can I help?" he asked.

She could think of an entire list of things she'd like to suggest to him from whisking her away from all this to seeing if he'd distract Ruth until they were sure Sammie Jo was all right. She settled for asking, "I don't suppose you sell helmets and knee and elbow pads in Aunt Sammie's size?"

"Sorry, no." He chuckled. "Besides, I don't know anyone brave enough to try to make her wear them."

"You got that right," her aunt shot back.

Emma pressed her fingers to the pulse point again. "Barring that, I don't suppose you'd know where I could get a blood-pressure kit?"

"I do! Got half a dozen, whatever you need. Just let me grab one." Ray Bob's heavy footsteps underscored his claim.

As he hurried off into another part of the store, Hank and Claire and Emma all called out at the same time, "A new one!"

"Of course a new one," Ray Bob hollered back. "Nothing but the best for Samantha Jolene."

In short order Emma had the tips of the stethoscope in her ears and the blood-pressure cuff secured around Sammie Jo's thin arm. She took the reading and sighed.

"Is it crazy high?" Claire circled them like a bird unable to find a place to perch.

"Actually, it's low." Emma spun the release valve between her thumb and forefinger and the cuff deflated with a long, hushed hiss.

"That's good, isn't it?" Sammie Jo planted her feet flat on the floor as if she expected to leap up and go right back to shopping.

"Not if it makes you go woozy and fall off ladders." Emma reached for the cuff and tugged it open. The hook and loop strip holding it in place gave a decisive ripping sound. "Is there any way we can get a call in to her doc—"

"Already dialed." Hank had the phone to

his ear. "He's a friend. I have his private number."

"Thanks," Emma murmured. "Just tell him —"

"Just tell him you won't be needing his services. I am fine." Sammie Jo shifted her weight, bracing one arm against the lowest shelf and thrusting her other hand up. "Would somebody help me get up? Ruth and I have a wish list to fill."

"Stay right where you are," Claire snapped, her anxiety showing.

"Just rest a minute," Emma cooed, not because she felt so much more serene but because she knew that as the authority on the scene, her remaining cool would help keep everyone else calm. She glanced up at Hank, who was now talking to the local M.D., and she couldn't help thinking of how he had pretty much tried to tell her the same thing in working with Ruth. Her actions set the tone. She was the one Ruth would look to and take her cues from.

Emma knew that, of course, but like most people she hadn't really applied what she knew and advised to others, to her own situation. She felt badly about that and resolved then and there to do better.

Sammie Jo lumbered up to her knees, wobbled to and fro then put her hand to her temple.

If only Ruth were Emma's only worry in that department. "Aunt Sammie . . ."

"Okay. I'll see to it myself." Hank paused then gave out a big laugh. "Are those doctor's orders, because I might just follow through on that suggestion."

"What suggestion?" Aunt Sammie eyed the man warily as she leaned heavily on Emma's shoulder.

Emma, Claire, Ray Bob and the bystanders all waited for Hank's reply with bated breath.

"He wants us to take your aunt to the hospital over in Port Elaine." He clicked his phone off with one thumb.

"I'm not going," Sammie said before he got the device slid back into his pocket.

"He said you'd say that. Furthermore, he said that *when* you said that I should feel free to give you a horse tranquilizer, load you into the back of my truck and haul you there myself, if that's what it took. But at all costs, I should get you to that hospital. He wants to run some tests."

"Tests? What tests? I don't need any tests. I'm fine." Sammie Jo struggled to her feet, took one indomitable step toward Ruth, reeled and staggered backward into the shelf. Her arm and back crashed into a display of small ceramic pots, sending them spilling.

One crashed to the floor and shattered into clunky shards at Ruth's feet.

Claire gasped.

Hank bent down and gathered up the small child and her large hat. He whisked Ruth away. "Hey, kiddo, let's go pay for all this stuff that you wanted and your great-aunt was gonna need anyway so we can take her for a ride."

"We?" Emma reached out to steady her aunt even as her brain rushed to piece together the logistics of their situation.

"Where we going?" Ruth asked as Hank settled her in front of the checkout counter. "In the wagon?"

"No wagon, not for this." Hank bent at the knees to try to keep eye contact with Ruth, even though Emma's daughter didn't cooperate. "We're going to take her to the doctor in another —"

Ruth cocked her head and finally looked at Hank. "Doctor Ben?"

Hank's eyes narrowed. "Doctor . . ."

"No, not Doctor Ben." Emma shut her eyes at the mention of the man she had walked out on in Atlanta a couple of days earlier. She did not need to take the emotional burden of thinking about Ben Weaver, his offer or the way she had left things with him.

"Dr. Ben once took an ugly bug out of the water in a place with fire on the tables and ate it." Ruth babbled out the most complete sentence Emma had ever heard her say to anyone who wasn't a close friend or family.

In other circumstances Emma would have been celebrating. But with Ruth talking about Ben *to* Hank while Emma tried to help her aunt move slowly through Ray Bob's store, it definitely drained Ruth's accomplishment of some excitement.

"He ate the fire?" Hank purposefully misunderstood.

Ruth giggled. "He ate the bug."

The sentence, the giggle, the proper comeback to a nonsensical remark. Any other time or with any other person and Emma would be singing.

"Ben? Is that the doctor you work for?" Claire had made her way around them and was standing at the counter with her wallet in hand.

"You work for a bug-eating doctor?" Hank straightened up to shift his curious gaze to Emma.

"It was a lobster, and that's not important now." Emma shook her head, as if that

137

could cast off all the questions, and changed the subject to something much more pertinent. "What matters right now is that we decide how we're going to get Aunt Sammie to Port Elaine."

"Wagon," Ruth said as if it were the most logical means of transportation available.

"Yes, take me in the little red wagon, Emma, honey." Sammie Jo crinkled her nose at Ruth. "We'll be over to the hospital by dinnertime then you can haul me back in the night and we can howl at the moon. Aaa-ooo."

"Aaa-ooo," Ruth echoed, holding the hat on her head and tipping it back. Head still back she seemed to ask the ceiling, "Can we fall in the boo-gun-veel-yas?"

"Oh, not only can we, darlin', I suspect it will be unavoidable." Sammie Jo gave Ruth's leg a jiggle to get the girl to drop her gaze. She didn't quite manage to make eye contact as she promised, "We will fall into them and come out with them on our hats and everyone will say —"

"Enough." Emma threw her hands up.

"Too-oo much," Ruth uttered low, with a sideways glance at her mother then her great-aunt.

"You're very funny, you two." Emma indulged her aunt and daughter with a smile. Her sense of urgency had quieted some as Sammie Jo's color was good, she was making sense — well, as much sense as usual — and she didn't show any signs of physical distress. "But let's be serious. We can't all take Aunt Sammie to the hospital."

"Aunt Sammie can come home." Ruth stretched to snag the watering can off the counter. "She can help me grow."

"I'm afraid you'll have to settle for me helping you grow." Claire finished paying Ray Bob, then tucked her wallet away and held her hand out to her niece.

"You?" Emma seized Ruth's hand instead. "Why you?"

"Because you're the nurse." Claire took Emma and Ruth by the wrists, gave a gentle tug to pull them apart, then slipped her own hand in Ruth's. "You said it yourself, you're the one who can see to Aunt Sammie. Hank can drive my car and take you two to Port Elaine. Ray Bob will load this stuff into Hank's truck, and Ruth and I will go out to the sanctuary."

"I can't leave Ruth!" Emma suddenly couldn't get a deep breath.

"You're not *leaving* Ruth. You're leaving Ruth *with me*." Claire curled Ruth's hand more tightly in her own. "I am perfectly capable of taking care of her until you get

Aunt Sammie settled and can get back. Then I'll take over sitting with her at the hospital."

"Sounds like a plan." Hank fished his keys out of his pocket, handed them to Claire and took her keys from her. He hooked his arm in Sammie Jo's. "The sooner we get you there the sooner you get home."

"I like your thinking." Sammie Jo outpaced him as they headed for the door. "Claire, stop in at the Good Neighbor Grocery and pick up something that you can keep warmed up in case we're late for dinner."

"Late for dinner?" Emma looked at her sister holding Ruth's hand and then at Aunt Sammie rushing off arm in arm with Hank.

"Chicken is always nice." Sammie Jo looked back at Hank. "Don't you think so, Hank? I could eat fried chicken hot or cold anytime, day or night."

"This is not decided," Emma whispered to her sister before she went after her aunt. "Aunt Sammie, you know you won't really be back home tonight, don't you? You won't get your results and be released until at least Monday, maybe later if they don't get answers right away."

"Monday?" Sammie Jo froze. She looked at Hank, then over her shoulder at Emma, then back at Hank. "But I can't leave the bird sanctuary unattended for days on end."

"Don't worry about it, Aunt Sammie," Claire called out after them. "Em is here now."

"I'm here *for* now," Emma corrected, shooting her sister a scolding look. "I can look after things, of course. Keep the bird feeders full and make small talk with any bird watchers that wander in, but —"

"Oh, honey, you have been away too long." Sammie Jo waved her hand then started for the door again, talking even faster than she walked. "It's so much more than that, especially this time of year. I have to get things ready for when the flocks return for winter. The back fence between the house and the pond needs nearly two dozen pickets replaced and the whole thing waterproofed. Those attic windows need the old paint stripped off, the rusty nails pulled out, to be sealed and then painted again. Wouldn't hurt to clear out some things from up there, too. That on top of the basic maintenance. Em can't do that on her own and look after Ruth."

"I'll pitch in, Sammie Jo." Hank hustled ahead and held the door open for the older woman. The sunlight came streaming in, making it hard for Emma to catch the nuances of his expression as he helped Sammie Jo out the door. "I think I might benefit from getting rid of things that no longer serve a purpose and mending fences."

"You have your practice." Emma still had not budged.

"I can pretty much run my office out of the sanctuary for a few days." He ran his hand back through his hair to clear it from his eyes then gave her a shrug. "No problem."

"That seems like an awfully big sacrifice on your part." She tucked a thin curl of pale blond hair up under Ruth's hat. "I don't want you to end up resenting having committed to all that."

"Not at all." He stood with one foot outside the door and one inside. He kept his hand on Sammie Jo's back and his eyes locked on Emma. "I've tested my limits in life, Emma. I know what I can do and when to step out and take a chance, to take on something new."

Was that a message to her about their relationship or a dig about what he saw as her overprotectiveness toward Ruth? Either way Emma could not let the challenge she found in his words go unanswered. "I came here to clear my head, to consider what I need to do, to test my own limits as it were."

She gave Ruth a kiss on the cheek, which the child pulled away from. Then settled for a pat on her leg, letting her hand trail along all the way to the sole of Ruth's shoe as she walked toward the door. "Aunt Sammie, don't you give another thought about the house or the bird sanctuary. You do whatever the doctor thinks you need to do to see to your health. I'll stay at the sanctuary as long as you need me to."

CHAPTER EIGHT

Emma sat in the backseat with Sammie Jo for the ride over, trying to get as much information out of the older woman as possible because she knew once they got to the hospital her aunt would be all "I'm fine," "there's no problem" and "I have no idea why I'm here."

Emma forgot to consider her aunt's additional agendas that had nothing to do with convincing health-care providers that she was just fine and dandy. Those took the form of: "My niece is a nurse, do you have a job for her here?" and "These two almost got married years ago, don't you think they make a cute couple?"

Every step of getting Sammie Jo admitted to the smallish but busy hospital wore away at Emma's already thin facade of holding it together.

Hank tried to smooth the way with that increasingly compelling and yet annoying way of his. Emma saw the wisdom in so much of what the man said and did. Yet time and again she wavered between gratitude for his being with her, wondering if he had always been this firm and insightful, and wishing that once in a while he'd give her a chance to say and do things her own way.

By the time they got the patient settled into her room and the list of things she wanted brought from home noted, Emma was exhausted.

"It's been a long day." Hank popped open the back door of Claire's oversize sedan and swept his hand out like a coachman offering Cinderella her carriage. "Care to climb in the backseat, curl up, catch up on some z's on the way home?"

Emma was exhausted, but not so exhausted she didn't have some fight left in her to finally get to do something her way. "I'm fine. Besides, if I take a nap this late in the day I'll never get to sleep tonight."

Brave last words.

They were pretty much the last thing she remembered until the truck came to a stop with a thud in the driveway of the migratory-bird sanctuary.

"Oh! Uh." She blinked to try to help orient herself as she looked out over the shapes of trees and moss and grasses altered by the dimming light of dusk. She pushed herself upright using the upholstered padding below the passenger-side window. When the edge of her palm pressed down against a damp spot, she immediately wiped the corner of her mouth then sheepishly worked up a weak smile. "I hope I didn't snore."

"Not any worse than I've heard before." Hank reached over and brushed the soft web of bedraggled brown hair curled against her cheek.

She covered her mouth with her hand, chagrined. "You mean no worse than when I snored the first day back?"

"No worse than I've heard out of my bulldog, Otis."

From behind them came a low woof, the only warning before Otis and Earnest T stuck their cold noses above the seat.

"I thought I just dreamed you stopping by your house to pick them up." She rubbed her eyes.

"If that's so, then you're a pretty grumpy dreamer. You groused and grumbled under your breath about needing to get back to Ruth the whole ten minutes it took for me to call the boys out to the car." He leaned close, smiled his heart-thumper of a smile then gave her a kiss on the forehead as natural as if all the years and issues that had separated them had never happened. "You kept telling me how anxious you were to see how Claire and Ruth got along. So here we are, go see."

"I — I will. Thanks." She gave her head a shake and brought herself back from wherever her mind had gone. Ruth. That was the important thing. She hopped out of the car and called for her child. "Ruth! Mommy's back!"

"Look! Look how many bugs I got!" Ruth dropped the butterfly net in the yard, picked up the Mason jar at her feet and came running down the walkway straight at Emma and Hank.

Emma rushed forward and got down on one knee, her arms spread wide to greet her sweet child.

Ruth went *clunk-ity-clunk* in her own kind of galloping right by Emma only to lift the jar aloft in both hands and shout, "Earnest T! Otis! Look at what bugs I got!"

The dogs that Hank had stopped by to pick up because he hated having left them kenneled most of the day sniffed at the jar in the epitome of doggy politeness.

"Well, I guess I know where I rank." Emma couldn't have been annoyed if she had tried. It felt too good to see Ruth so filled with joyous enthusiasm about anything, even if it didn't include telling her mom how much she'd been missed today.

The dogs got more enthusiastic. Tails thumping and entire bodies wriggling, they pressed in on Ruth, trying to get to the jar.

Ruth squealed.

Emma gripped Hank's arm to get up quickly.

"Take charge, Ruth. Tell them no." He put up his hand to stop Emma from running to Ruth's aid. "Turn your back to them. Show them you're the boss and you won't let them push you around."

Emma sank her teeth into her lower lip but gave Hank's way a chance to work. She had only been apart from Ruth for about five hours, but it had seemed forever. Knowing Ruth wasn't just another town over, but that far away *and* back at their old home with Claire, raised in their aunt's old ways, Emma couldn't help feeling the all-too-often ill-equipped little girl was practically in another world. Now, waiting to see how Ruth handled the situation, all those anxieties rose in her again.

The dogs got too nosey with her a second time. Earnest T pushed at the jar with his nose and the bulldog, Otis, woofed softly and crowded in so close the child had to keep moving to keep from stepping on him or tripping over him.

"No. I'm the boss of dogs." Ruth put her back to the two dogs.

The animals snuffled and tried to get around her.

"Keep your back to them," Hank called. "You're doing it just right."

Ruth shifted to keep her back to the dogs and they calmed down.

"Look at her." Emma's fingers closed around the rolled-back sleeve of Hank's shirt. "She's doing what you told her to do. Good job, Ruth, that's the way to not give the dogs attention for bad behavior."

Ruth grinned at her as if she'd just noticed her mom was even on the premises. "I got bugs. I'm the boss of dogs."

"You are, sweetie. You sure are." Emma's heart soared to see the small triumph her daughter had achieved.

"Makes you feel kinda silly having worried about her so much all afternoon, doesn't it?" Hank stood on the walkway, positioned so that he could talk to Emma but keep a vigilant eye on his dogs and her daughter.

"I didn't . . ." Emma stopped herself. She couldn't lie. She dropped her gaze to the shoes she'd borrowed from Aunt Sammie's closet. "Guess I didn't do a very good job of concealing my anxiety, did I?"

"I whooshed them up with a net. Aunt Claire showed me how to crawl them up my finger and into the jar. I'm gonna get more to light up when it gets dark." Ruth bent forward to speak directly to the curious canines. "Wanna help?"

The dogs wagged their tails and wound their way around Ruth as she stood on one foot and then the other, holding her lightning-bug lantern up high in both hands. Earnest T, the bigger, shaggier one, nuzzled her neck and she shrieked in delight. "Don't get me! *I'm* not a bug!"

"Play gentle, boys," Hank admonished as the dogs went bounding off into the yard behind the child.

"Same for you, Ruthie," Emma didn't hesitate to add. "Don't you swoop that net around too wild and whap those dogs. They won't like it."

"Not swooping. Whooshing." Ruth demonstrated by trailing the net almost gracefully along behind her as she moved through the dusky yard glittered with the twinkle of lightning bugs flashing their "hellos" to one another.

"If the boys get too worked up, I can always call them down." Hank closed his hand around hers in reassurance.

Emma's heart did its own whoosh, or perhaps it was a full-on swoop, at the tenderness in his touch, in his voice, in the culmination of all the kindness he had shown today. This was not the callow young man she had given up on as husband material all those years ago.

This was a real man. A godly man. A man who was looking deeply into her eyes, holding her hands and leaning down to give her the kind of kiss that could change the way she felt about pretty much everything she had once thought she knew everything about.

"Emma . . ."

"What?"

His dark eyes searched her face. "I — I'm not sure if . . ."

"My whole life has been about not being sure, Hank," she whispered as she moved in so close that the breeze blew the loose tendrils of her braid to brush over his sleeve. She raised up on her toes. "Never sure what to do, where to go, what's best for Ruth. It's kept me scared and alone in ways I am only now beginning to understand."

He pulled her hands, still clasped in his, to his chest between them. "But you're sure about this?"

She tipped her head up, welcoming his

lips on hers. "Just for this one heartbeat out of time maybe it's okay not to be sure. Just for now, let's be —"

"Too-oo much!" Ruth shouted at the top her lungs.

Emma flinched, whipping her head around to see if everything was all right.

Ruth waved the net around. The larger of the two dogs leaped and spun in the air snapping at the bugs around them. "Go, Earnest T! Bite those bugs so I can get 'em!"

Emma relaxed, and laying her forehead against Hank's chest, laughed away the twist of tension the surprise had spurred in her.

"You were saying?" Hank lowered his head to speak softly against her cheek.

She closed her eyes and soaked in the comfort of having him so near, his warmth, his strength, the sweet memory of how much she had once loved him, how much she had been prepared to trust and rely upon him. She wanted all that and more in her life again. But did she honestly want it from Hank?

She stepped back and looked up at him. "I was saying, I think I've already said too much."

"Too-oo much," Ruth called out again. "Look at all the lightning bugs! Even me and Otis and Earnest T can't catch 'em all!"

"She sure has been a chatterbox today," Claire called out as she stood up and leaned against the wrought-iron handrail of the outer steps.

Emma jerked her hands free from Hank's, only then realizing her sister must have been sitting on the bottom step watching Ruth . . . and Hank and Emma . . . the whole time.

"I . . . um . . . I guess she's pretty wound up." She put both her hands behind her back, realizing even as she did it that it made her look as if she was trying to hide something. Still, she couldn't help herself. She spun around and quickly started putting distance between her and Hank.

Out in the yard Ruth squealed again.

Emma walked purposefully toward her older sister, babbling nervously about what she considered a safe subject. "You know, Ruth has always been highly verbal. Big vocabulary, but she only talks on her terms. It's pretty rare she ever goes on this much with anyone but me. You must have made a special connection with her today."

"Looks to me like I'm not the only one of the Newberry sisters that made a special connection today," Claire said just as Emma got close enough that she could speak softly enough for Hank not to overhear. "I'll expect details later."

A sharp dog bark in the background punctuated her sister's nosiness.

"There *are* no details and you'll be in Port Elaine with Aunt Sammie later," Emma managed to say in a whisper through a clenched jaw.

"Anxious to get rid of me so you and Hank can be alone?" Claire's eyes sparked with fun at teasing her younger sister.

"Hank is hitting the road before you even get Aunt Sammie's suitcase packed." She dug into the pocket of her jeans and thrust the list their aunt had dictated into her sister's hand. "There's no reason for him to hang around here."

More barking, more chatter from Ruth, a bit louder and more frenetic. *Was that a growl?*

"Looked to me like you were giving the man a reason to hang around."

"*The man* is just a . . . a . . . guy who happened by when I was . . . He's the town vet, and a family friend. That's all. Don't even joke that I want to be alone with him, Claire. It's not funny," Emma practically shouted, caught off guard by being caught in the near kiss — or was it just her imagination that Hank had wanted to kiss her? — and her embarrassment deepened. She glanced over her shoulder at the man she had sort of insulted. "Not that I don't truly appreciate all that you've —"

Hank met her gaze, shook his head then turned his back to her.

She deserved that. She was certainly not acting in a way anyone would want to encourage.

"Earnest T! Otis! Cool it." He snapped his fingers.

Emma's attention swung to her daughter and Hank's pets.

The dogs lay down in the grass obediently.

Ruth hugged the jar of lightning bugs to her chest, looking a bit guilty for having egged the animals on. "I didn't mean for them to get in trouble."

"It's okay, kiddo." Hank strode into the ankle-high grass to a few feet of Ruth, then bent forward, his hands on the knees of his jeans. "Using discipline is not the same as getting in trouble. Animal parents even use it to teach their little ones how to stay safe and still grow and learn and go out into the world."

"*I* can grow." Ruth's eyes lit up as if she had suddenly truly understood the width and breadth of something she'd been proclaiming all day long.

"Not only can you grow, you *will* grow, kiddo." Hank straightened up and looked back at Emma. "What you learn and how you go out into the world, I guess that depends on a lot of things."

Even the evening breezes seemed to still then.

Neither Hank nor Emma said a word.

Ruth looked as if she was waiting for someone to give her the signal that it was okay to move again.

"Hey, it's going to be dark enough soon to hang up that lantern," Claire chimed in a bit too cheerfully. She picked her way out into the grass to Ruth and offered her hand. "Bring it up to the porch and by the time you help me pack Aunt Sammie's suitcase, you can use it to light the way to my car."

She led Ruth away from the dogs, who watched but did not try to follow.

When Claire reached Hank she noted, "You must have worked with those dogs a lot to get them to react so well."

"Good dogs." Hank gave a quick nod to the animals then called out to Claire as she walked away with Ruth. "Work, yeah, but mostly, it's consistency."

"Consistency," Emma echoed. In a word, that was something her life had always lacked. From her upbringing to her own hectic world as a single mom, moving from nursing job to nursing job always hoping the money or the schedule would help her finally figure out how to provide for Ruth financially and to have time to tend to her child's mental, emotional and spiritual needs.

But where had Emma ever learned consistency? She had gone from the chaos of having lost her parents to the recklessly ordered lifestyle of Sammie Jo's bird sanctuary. Just as Ruth had had a moment of insight in realizing she could grow, Emma was having one now. She realized that in all her ups and downs of these past few years, even the one that made her run back to Gall Rive, she had been seeking this one thing. Consistency.

She watched Claire march hand in hand with Ruth, the glowing jar tucked under her arm, toward the porch.

"That's the key, isn't it? Training dogs. Teaching a child about life, the Lord and limitations." She raised her head to scan the horizon beyond the huge house. The moss gently stirred in the live oaks. The scent of grass and water drifted over them and she thought of how the day had begun for her and Hank. "Even scaring away a misplaced great blue heron."

"I don't know." At last he looked her way. "You start showing up regularly in that bird's territory he might just —"

"I know, I know, get used to it," she finished for him.

"I was going to say, he might just begin to look forward to it," he said quietly.

"Oh." She touched her braid. She glanced back in the direction of the pond. She wondered if the fading sunlight hid the color of the heat she felt rising in her cheeks standing here alone on the walk where she had practically begged Hank to kiss her moments ago. "Yeah, I guess a person — or a bird — could, uh, form attachments to someone they counted on every day, even for a short time."

The front door slammed shut with Claire and Ruth on the other side. They left the Mason jar resting on the bottom step.

"I need to remember to set those bugs free before I go to bed tonight." Emma watched the shimmering creatures flit and fly around in their eleven-ounce world. "Ruth may not like it, but maybe it can be another kind of lesson — that there are some things you shouldn't get attached to. Some things aren't meant to last."

"I guess I'd better get going if I plan to be outta here before Claire gets that suitcase ready." Hank's boots scuffed against the concrete walkway as he took a backward step and jerked his thumb toward his truck over his shoulder. "Sammie Jo said something about needing to get some work done around here? Cleaning up in the attic? Mending fences?"

"I hate to impose on you."

"You're not imposing."

"Oh, well . . ."

"Your aunt is." He stretched his arms out then fit his hand to his back and groaned. "And trust me, she has no issues imposing on me to get things done around here."

Emma laughed. It felt good. "That sounds like Aunt Sammie."

"So what works for you? Tomorrow after church?" He started to walk to the truck in earnest.

"Great." She looked back in the direction of the pond then headed down the walk after Hank. "Can we start with the fence first?"

"Sure. I'll bring my tool chest." He tightened his lips over his teeth and gave a quick whistle blast and made a hand gesture for the dogs. They hopped up and came running.

"Thanks. I'll feel better once it's done. It adds an extra layer of protection between

Ruth and the pond."

"The other layers being?" He swung open the door of the truck. The light from the cab of the vehicle put him in a warm halo.

"The other layer being, well, me. Watching over her every minute."

He made another gesture and the dogs clamored up onto the seat then wiggled their way behind that seat and settled in. "That sounds exhausting, Emma, and not really a long-term solution."

"I don't really need a . . ." She shut her mouth and looked back at the house. She was going to say she didn't need a long-term solution since she wasn't going to be around long-term but that protest had grown thin over the course of this day. Hank had been trying to get her to think beyond her stay here, beyond the immediate realities of Ruth right now. If she had learned anything from her hasty flight, her aunt's need for help and finding Hank in her life again, even if only for a very short time, it was that she had a lot more to learn. "What did you have in mind?"

He leaned one shoulder against the door and smiled at her.

Her stomach did a little flip-flop.

"You need to give Ruth the skills she needs to be around the pond, around this whole place." He looked up at the house, his head tipped back. "You need to teach her to be smart, not scared. It's the best thing —" he climbed into the cab and just before he shut the door added "— for both of you."

"Smart, not scared," she murmured as she watched him drive away.

It was certainly something to think about. Emma, however, suspected she'd have a hard time getting that near kiss out of her mind, and she couldn't help but wonder what that said about her, about the decision that had driven her here, a decision she had yet to make. It would all be so much easier if she had her own built-in layers of protection against the way that Hank Corsaut made her feel. If she didn't find some soon, she was afraid . . .

"Smart not scared," she repeated. "Smart not scared." She'd just keep telling herself that and hope it sank in before she saw him again tomorrow.

CHAPTER NINE

"Why does it bother you so much?" Hank paused to demand of Emma as she stood with the whole of her attention focused on the great blue heron perched at the edge of the Newberrys' pond.

"Did I say it bothered me?" She spoke to him with her face in profile, unwilling to take her eyes off the heron for a minute or to look directly at Hank.

He had stopped home long enough after church to change out of his dress clothes and into a ragged, faded pair of jeans and a T-shirt so worn and thin that when he snagged the sleeve on one of the wooden pickets he had moved from the truck bed to near the fence, he simply tore that sleeve, then the other one, completely off.

As soon as he'd arrived he'd driven his truck around the house into the back alongside the broken and weathered fence that separated the yard proper from the property with the pond. Finished with the pickets, he closed the tailgate of his old truck again. Over the metallic creaking of it slamming into place, he asked her, "Why can't you let it go, then?"

"I'd love to but the crazy thing *won't* go." She narrowed her eyes to steely slits, pointed two fingers to her eyes then at the bird to let the creature know she was watching. Then she made a motion like a bird taking flight with both her hands, all done for Hank's benefit, to lighten the mood. "Believe me, I'm not trying to stop it."

"You know what I mean." Hank pulled the toolbox from the truck and carted it to the pile of pickets stacked beside the weathered fence. He dropped the metal tool chest to the ground with a decisive clang and thump. "It's not about the bird with you, is it?"

Emma flinched slightly. She hadn't expected Hank to be so direct or to not simply let it all go. Why did he care, anyway? Shouldn't it be enough that the bird upset her? She folded her hands together but she did not look away from the bird.

It shifted away from them with a few sideways steps.

"I told you, Ruth is drawn to that heron. It's big and close in ways no other birds

163

are, even around this place. She can see the connection between it and the origami paper cranes she loves to make." Emma made a delicate gesture with her thumbs and forefingers, miming the final folds of the paper bird to form the long neck and pointed beak. "The whole time we've been here I keep thinking . . . Okay, you've got me. It's not just about the bird."

Emma shut her eyes, weary from carrying her anxiety, too. It wasn't realistic of her to think Hank wouldn't press her for answers. He had been pushing her to think about her motives and choices since she first fell out of her SUV and into his world again two days ago. "It's about what the bird represents."

He crouched to gather a buttery-colored leather tool belt from the tool chest. With that in one hand and a hammer in the other, he stood and fastened it low-slung around his hips. "And just what does that bird represent to you, Em?"

She studied the heron from the curve of its long neck to the dusty, deep tones of its blue-gray plumage. She could see the craggy bumps and bulges along its stick-thin legs and saw the rise and fall of its rapid breathing.

She moved to the open space where some

of the rotten pickets had already been removed from the fence and placed her hands on the top connection rail. "I imagine that God looks at us, His children, sometimes, the same way I see that great blue heron."

He slid the hammer into its sling, then reached down to pick up a pair of torn and dirty canvas gloves. He tugged them on and flexed his fingers. "You've lost me."

She turned to find him swinging a picket over his shoulder. Hank Corsaut was here, at her family home after all these years. She *had* lost him but now here he was in her life again, if only at the edge of it, and only for a while. "Well, I mean that God knows the rhythm of the seasons."

"Of course, He created them." He moved to the open space next to her and lowered the picket into place.

"Yes, and He knows the intricacies of our hearts, which He also created."

He positioned the picket so that the top and bottom matched perfectly with the one on the other side of it. "With you so far."

"So He knows the way that we should go. It says in Psalms that as our shepherd, He directs our paths."

"Uh-huh." He pulled out a nail, squinted

at it, then plunked it back into the box at his feet.

"But so many times so many of His children think they know better." Emma really was going somewhere with this but since she wasn't exactly sure where, she appreciated Hank not forcing her to rush to a conclusion. "Or they want something so badly they convince themselves that they know what God wants."

He leaned the new picket against the old fence and looked at her. "They refuse to listen to His counsel and end up straying off course, end up alone and lost."

"Well, some would argue that because God loves us we are never really alone," she hedged.

"Are you lost, Emma? Is that why you showed up here after running all night?" He pulled his glove off and put his hand to her cheek. "Is that what this is all about?"

His touch warmed her like the sun on her face and lifted her heart like the wind in her hair. "Not lost so much as . . ."

"Afraid the next step you take might be the one that pulls you off course?" he asked.

The next step might be the one that pulls you off course, or puts your feet on the right path at last. She kept that thought to herself.

She slid her hands into her pockets and

her fingertips brushed over her phone. She thought of all the unanswered messages that Ben Weaver had left every day since she'd run off. Maybe she should just go inside and call him, get it over with. But would that be the step that helped her or made her falter? She just didn't know.

"Emma?"

"Hmm?" She tilted her head up. "Oh. I, um, I guess I was trying to go all deep and philosophical there when really, what I meant to say was, I came back to Gall Rive not even sure what I expected and found this great blue heron here and I instantly felt . . ." She bent low and stepped over the lower rail in the hole in the fence, swinging her upper body through the opening. She began to walk cautiously toward the pond. "Well, you know how when a child grows up and moves away, they call those parents empty nesters?"

"Yeah. Sure." Hank followed behind her, ducking under the top rail and walking softly through the tall grass. When she held her hand up to bring him to a stop, he obliged her. "What about it?"

"Well, that won't be me." She cocked her head to one side, trying to determine if this heron was ill or injured. "I will always have a little bird with a broken wing in my nest."

"But, Emma, you don't know . . . There are all sorts of . . ."

"It's okay, Hank." Again she held her hand up. "I'm just trying to figure out what path God would have me take, what's the best thing for my wounded bird of a girl, and I can't help looking at this heron and feeling . . ." Guilt. Empathy. Vulnerability. Fear. "So sad."

His feet swished through the grass behind her. "Ruth is not like that —"

"I know. I know." She put her hands out and tossed her hair back. "Let's not belabor it. Especially when we've got so much labor we should be laboring at right here with this fence."

Hank threw his head back and groaned but to his credit he let her get away with the crummy pun and with not allowing him to finish his reasonable conclusion. "All right. Let's get to it. It shouldn't take more than an hour."

"An hour?" She shaded her eyes with her hand and assessed the length of the busted-up fence then gave him a discerning once-over from the tool belt to the torn shirt. "Is that all?"

He held up one finger then went sprinting off to his truck. He leaned into the cab, clattered and clunked around a bit then

168

emerged wearing eye protection and carrying a nail gun. He stood there a moment giving her a great view of him in full tool-guy gear, the wind ruffling his black hair and his grin telling her he was a man to be reckoned with.

"What was all that with the nails and hammer and . . . ? You had me worrying about Aunt Sammie overworking you!"

"Hey, you can still worry if you want. It's still work." He strode to the fence, lined up a picket and punched it into place via the ear-splitting *ka-chunk ka-chunk* of the nail gun. Once it was in place he stepped back to show off his achievement. "I learned a long time ago that whenever dealing with the Newberry family, always give yourself whatever edge possible."

She had to laugh at that. She sure couldn't argue with it. She clapped her hands together. "So what is there for me to do?"

"I'm going to line the pickets up next to the ones that need replacing. As I get to each one you can hold the new picket straight while I nail it in place."

And that's what they did for the better part of the next hour. Worked together as a team, though he could have done just fine without her.

"Y'all ready for a break?" Claire came

around the side of the house with a big silver tray covered by a yellow-and-green tea towel.

"We have pink cake and pink lemonade." Ruth planted her feet a few inches away from Hank and looked up at him. "Real cake."

"It's amazing what you can do with food coloring and maraschino-cherry juice," Claire muttered out of the corner of her mouth.

Emma didn't even make a remark about how her sister could do amazing things with just about anything. She whisked one of the ice-cold glasses off the tray and pressed it to her hot, damp neck.

"That looks great." Hank grabbed a glass as well and rolled it across his sweaty forehead.

"All that trouble to make lemonade and we could have just brought them ice packs," Claire told Ruth.

"Where is Earnest T and Otis?" Ruth began to creep about in the tall grass, peering high and low.

"I let them stay at my house because it wouldn't be safe for them to come out here with us working." He took a drink and made it look so refreshing that Emma had to gulp some of the pretty pink liquid down from her own glass.

"That's okay." Ruth perked up, whirled around and began her uneven clomping run full tilt toward the pond. She shouted, "I'll just pet my bird-friend instead."

Emma reacted so quickly that she spilled her drink all over herself. The chill took her breath away and kept her from screaming at Ruth in a fit of panic.

Claire gasped and stepped backward.

Hank took the opportunity to take Emma by the arm. "The fence is done. The gate hinges are practically rusted shut. You can get to her before she gets to the heron. You have time to think about how you really want to handle this."

She spun her head around and their eyes met. Emma did not need Hank to teach her how to be a parent, but she had known for a very long time that she needed at least a second set of eyes to help her see her child from other angles, to point out to her the things she couldn't see by being so close to the situation. And here were those eyes, looking into her. This was the test. This was the time for her to choose her course.

She whisked the sticky, dripping liquid from her clothes and chin and said, loud enough to be heard but calm enough to be taken quite seriously, "Not so fast, young lady. I have a question to ask you before you go running off."

Ruth slowed as she reached the fence. She put one hand on the gate latch but she did not try to open it.

Emma set the glass back on the tray and headed out across the yard to her child.

Ruth turned where she stood and waited for Emma to get to her.

"I told you not to bother that bird. It's a wild creature and you running at it like that is going to scare it." Emma got to the gate and bent at the knees to speak directly to her daughter. "You ever had a time when someone came running at you, making a lot of noise?"

"Yes." Ruth nodded then slowly unfurled her index finger to point directly at Emma. "You."

Ouch. Emma couldn't pretend that that didn't hurt. But it also proved Hank's point and Emma's own wisdom about staying cool in a time of crisis being the best way to help others. Emma took a deep breath and squinted to keep the sun and the twinge of tears from blurring her vision.

She threw an anxious look Hank's way.

He pointed to his chest then to the mother and daughter by the fence, his way of asking Emma if he could approach.

She nodded and as he came close, she smoothed one hand down the T-shirt that Aunt Sammie had bought at Ray Bob's with a cartoon cat on it. "Okay. Yes. I know I've been kind of . . . yelly lately."

"Too-oo much," Ruth informed her.

Hank crooked a "she told *you*" eyebrow at Emma but held his tongue.

"I know. With you not doing well in your school last year and having to decide what to do about that, I know I did not act very well at times. But you know Mommy never meant it to hurt you, right?"

Never ask Ruth a question unless you are prepared for the answer. Emma held her breath.

Ruth stroked her mother's face and laughed. "You're all sticky."

That was as close as she'd probably get to an answer right now so Emma pressed on. "So when Mommy yelled and ran after you, even though she was trying to do something good for you, how did it make you feel?"

Ruth frowned. She wasn't really good at expressing feelings. She often tended to try to just parrot back the feelings she thought others wanted to see in her.

Emma considered that for a moment and decided to go "Hank" on her child, direct but empathetic. "Let me put it this way, did you like it?"

Ruth shook her head.

"Do you think that bird would like it if you did that to it?"

Another head shake.

"You going to leave the bird alone now?"

Ruth screwed her lips over to one side. She curled one finger in her hair and yanked at the butterfly clip Claire must have used to hold her bangs back.

Emma put her hand on Ruth's to still the angsty and self-destructive behavior.

Ruth went still. She looked over her shoulder toward the bird and sighed. "Bye-bye, bird-friend."

"Good . . . choice," Emma said, picking her words carefully.

"You, too, Mom," Hank murmured, leaning close.

"I have to say, y'all look like one sweet little family standing out here by the picket fence like that." Claire, having left the tray on the back porch, came strolling up with a big grin on her face.

Emma gave her sister a warning look, stood and took Ruth by the hand. "This little family is going to go clean up so we can go visit the rest of our family, Aunt Sammie. And I think Hank needs to get back to *his* family, Otis and Earnest T."

Hank started to say something then just closed his mouth, shook his head and turned to head toward the house.

"Can I just go play in the water?" Ruth looked back longingly.

"It's not very clean." Claire made a sour face and shook her head. "You might catch a bug."

"I like catching bugs." Ruth kicked at the grass as they walked.

"Not this kind." They reached the point where Hank needed to go one way to get into his truck and they needed to go another to go into the house.

Hank paused and leaned down to say to Ruth, "Maybe you can get your friend Ben to come out here and deal with those bugs for you."

"Blech." Ruth wrinkled her nose.

"Let's go inside and get ready to go see Aunt Sammie." Claire took Ruth's hand.

"Not funny," Emma said, meaning that on so many levels. The old guilt pang at not having spoken to Ben made her stiffen up as she tried to conclude things with Hank. "So, um, thank you for . . . the fence and . . . a lot more, you know."

"Yeah. No problem. I'm glad to do whatever I can for —"

"Can't play with my dog-friends. Can't

play with my bird-friend." Ruth counted out the growing list of things she couldn't do with every stomping step. "Can't go in the attic. Can't go to the water. Can't go . . . I can go in the down part?"

"Only if there's a bad storm," Emma called out after her. "Only go in the basement to stay safe from wind and rain, thunder and lightning."

"Yes!" Ruth shot her fist into the air. "I can pray for storms! I can go in the base-a-ment and fall in the boo-gun-veel-yas. Aaa-ooo."

Hank laughed, then turned to Emma and jerked his head toward the house. "Speaking of going in the attic, I have a packed schedule tomorrow but I'll come back and work on those windows on Tuesday."

"Oh, Hank, you shouldn't take any more time away from your work to pitch in around here."

"It's okay. I always keep the day after cat clinic free to, um, lick my wounds."

"Cat clinic?"

"You know how it is with country people and cats, they don't tend to get them regular care. So I set aside one day a month so people can bring their cats in for routine stuff, shots, trim their nails, spay and neutering by appointment, that kind of thing. Of course, I'll always see a cat in an emergency, but if people know I've cleared my schedule for a whole day they are better about coming in with their animals. It's easier for some of them and a whole lot easier for me."

"Cats? Easy?" She folded her arms and leaned back against his truck.

"The little ones aren't so tough," he said, cupping his hands to indicate the size of a small kitten.

Emma couldn't help it. The idea of those work-roughened hands taking care of a helpless kitten got to her. The man got to her, from his sense of humor to his practical way of dealing with everything from Aunt Sammie to Ruth. If she wasn't still sticky from spilling lemonade, she thought she might just go up on tippy toe and place a kiss on his cheek.

"So, Tuesday, then?" he asked.

"It's a date." She paused mid nod. "No, not a date . . . but . . . a Tuesday! I'll be here."

CHAPTER TEN

"Cooler today with mostly sunny skies. Things could change by early afternoon when a shift in the wind brings —"

"Nonsense." Hank pressed the mute button and tossed the remote control onto the bed. He hadn't really been watching the small TV hanging above his chest of drawers anyway. He'd been spending more of his energy trying to ignore the accusatory gazes of Otis and Earnest T reflected at him in the bathroom mirror. He'd resorted to voicing his thoughts when he couldn't completely block them out, which was *not* the same as talking to the animals. "I am not doing this to impress her."

The dogs, who had draped themselves over the foot of his bed in order to get a better look at him going to extra pains to get ready this morning, huffed and groaned as if to say, "You can protest all you want but you're not foolin' us, pal."

"When I want your opinions, I'll ask for them." Hank dragged a brand-new razor over the last remaining cloud of shaving cream on his cheek, then leaned in to make sure he'd gotten every last whisker. "And since I don't hold conversations with pets, don't expect to hear me asking for those opinions anytime soon, much less taking said opinions to heart."

Otis hefted his ponderous bulldog body up, made a tight circle and put his backside to Hank. He aimed a droopy-eyed scowl over his well-padded shoulder, gave a jowly snort, then slumped down again.

A politician with a team of word-wrangling speech writers working overtime could not have expressed disgust at Hank's declaration more eloquently.

Hank shook the blob of shaving cream off the razor and into the sink, flicked on the water and rinsed the blade end off. After taking way too long at that, he finally tossed the razor onto the counter. "Okay, okay. I admit it. I like the woman."

Earnest T's tail whapped against the bedspread but that in no way indicated if he approved of Hank's sentiment or just liked hearing his master's voice.

"Why is that such a shocker?" Steam began to rise as hot water gushed to fill the small sink in his small master bath. Hank jerked free the towel he'd had slung over his shoulder and began to wipe his face clean. "Once upon a time I actually *loved* her. Wanted to marry her. But . . ."

Hank paused and faced his hazy image in the now-foggy mirror. "I got scared."

He searched the blurry image before him. He was no longer talking to the animals so conveniently within earshot. This confession, finally spoken aloud, was for his own conscience. It was, in his own often awkward but heartfelt way, a means of laying it all before the Lord in hopes that he might do as he and Emma had talked about, find the way he was supposed to go.

"I had such a lousy childhood. I just couldn't imagine bringing children into a world where they were so helpless and could be hurt so easily." He breathed the warm, damp air into his lungs, held it, then let it out slowly. Wadding up the towel to find a place free of shaving cream, he reached out and wiped the mirror, creating an oval big enough to see his own face clearly. "But then it was that helplessness and hurt that brought me to You, Lord. That showed me where to put my trust."

He shut his eyes and murmured a thank-you. He followed that with a request that he not forget his own frailties as he dealt with others, especially Emma and Ruth, then eased an amen out with a sigh and straightened up.

The movement made Earnest T cock his head in curiosity.

Hank tucked the towel into the rack and laughed. "So, you got me. I like Emma. I like her in ways I wasn't mature enough to appreciate when we were younger. And that Ruth?"

Earnest T's ears pricked up.

"That kid gets to me." He flipped off the bathroom light, strode into the bedroom and gave Earnest T a scratch behind the ears. "Figures, doesn't it?"

The animal leaned into Hank's touch. The roughness of his fur grated against the dozen or so tiny scratches covering his fingers and palm, compliments of yesterday's patient load. "Me and my unlikely causes. Cat clinics. Safety helmets for kids learning to ride ponies. Rescuing stray dogs. Staying in a place where I have to spread my services all over the county to make a decent living. Spending my free time trying to tame those Newberry women."

He had meant the last part as a joke, trying to lighten his own mood, but as he moved to his dresser to grab a fresh T-shirt he realized it had done just the opposite.

The dogs seemed to pick up on his preoccupation. Otis thumped down off the end of the bed and waddled over to butt his massive head against the hem of Hank's jeans.

"Yeah, it is kinda like beating my head against an immovable object, boy. But I have to do it. They need me." He slipped the T-shirt over his head and tugged it into place. "Ruth needs a calm, stable influence of a person who won't spoil her or try to keep her wrapped in cotton so nothing can ever harm her. And Emma . . ."

Her name caught in his throat. She had gotten under his skin, maybe not in the same way she had all those years ago, but in a new, maybe more significant way. A way that Hank wasn't ready to explore or even acknowledge completely. Not to Otis or Earnest T, not even to himself.

"Emma needs me right now the way birds need Sammie Jo's place. Emma needs me to be a sanctuary, a safe place to land, to rest, to take refuge from the storm. Not a forever kind of thing, just for . . ." He started for the door, then turned back to use Emma's own words to remind himself of the situation, of the course they were both on and where it would eventually lead.

182

"Just for this one heartbeat out of time, Emma needs me and I intend to be there for her."

He gave the hand signal and called for the dogs to go into their kennels. As he slid the bar into the slot to shut the latch, the scratches and cuts on his fingertips made him wince. If he intended to spend the day gripping a paint brush or sanding window frames he had better have a better pair of work gloves than the ones he had kept too long in his old tool chest.

He was waiting outside Ray Bob's when the store's namesake showed up to unlock the doors but it was someone else's arrival that had him climbing out of his old truck so fast he nearly stumbled and did a face-plant into the road.

"Sammie Jo Newberry! Don't tell me you bashed some poor nurse's aide over the head with a bedpan, fashioned a rope from your bedsheets and made a harrowing escape from the hospital." He waved as he hollered to be heard all the way into the Good Neighbor Grocery's parking lot.

"I did no such thing!" Sammie Jo bellowed right back at him, managing to convey her indignity at his very suggestion before she folded her arms smugly over her thin upper body and kicked up her chin to strike a defiant pose. "They got thoroughly fed up hearing from me about all the ways they could improve the care and the food around the place that one of 'em came in yesterday afternoon, yanked out the IV and turned me loose on society again."

"I'm sure they miss you already," he teased.

"Well, I wouldn't bet on them taking up a collection to buy bus tickets anytime soon to come out and pay me a visit, if that tells you anything," Sammie Jo called out before she poked her elbows out and did a little jig as if to celebrate the kind of feisty attitude that had earned her an early release. "Nice seeing ya, Hank. Emma tells me you're heading out our way to get to work on those windows today. I'll pick up something special here in the grocery to whip you up for lunch as a means of saying thank you! See you back at the house."

"I'll probably be out there before you are," Hank called back.

"Not before me! 'Cuz I'm gonna fly!" Ruth popped out onto the sidewalk from between two parked cars, her arms straight out like wings.

Hank hurried forward, both hands out, to tell her not to run into the street.

Before he said a word, Emma called out

firm, but cool, "Stop right there, young lady. Wait for me to get there to show you how to cross that street."

Just the sound of her voice made Hank smile.

She came around the silver SUV that he now recognized as the one he'd seen her careening home in less than a week ago. Then, in her fancy clothes and diamonds she had seemed practically a stranger to him, despite their history. Now as he took in the sight of the sun on her face, her hair loose and windblown, wearing old jeans she'd probably left in the house years ago and a Gall Rive High School T-shirt with the faded mascot, the Gall Rive Gator, on the front, it felt as if she'd only been away a few days. Hours maybe. In his heart she still seemed young and hopeful and ready to take on anything or anyone.

Without looking around, Emma wound her way over to Ruth and took the child by the hand. "Gall Rive doesn't have crosswalks but that doesn't mean you can just run across the street anywhere. Let's go down to the corner."

He leaned his forearms against the open window of his open door and just watched as Emma patiently schooled the little girl in the proper way to get from one side of the street to the other. The oppressive heat of the past few days had let up a little. The wind stirred enough to set the American flag outside the post office waving. Off to the east, fat, sun-brightened clouds gathered. It looked and felt as if it was shaping up to be a perfect day.

Made all the more perfect by the company he expected to keep. Though he couldn't hear Emma talking he could see how she bent to speak to the child and encouraged Ruth to mimic her actions — looking both ways, watching the signal, moving quickly across the street.

The pair came up the sidewalk in front of Ray Bob's toward him and Hank stepped away from the truck and let the door fall shut with a *wham.* "Nice job, kiddo."

Emma jumped. "You scared me."

"Believe me, that's the last thing I'd ever want to do." He met her on the sidewalk. "Next time I'll do something to make sure you know I'm here."

"Next time *I'm* doing it without hands," Ruth announced to him, turning loose of her mother's hand. She held her own hands up and out as if Hank needed to see them to understand the magnitude of the freedom she intended to enjoy.

"Good for you," he said softly, wondering

if he had ever felt that sure and happy at the same time. He turned his eyes to Emma and it hit him that he had felt that way, too briefly, too long ago when she had first said she would marry him.

"Darting into traffic and not watching for cars in parking lots have both been huge issues for us. I've yelled and hovered over her and told her not to leave my side but I didn't see she was ready to be given the privilege of actually doing it herself until . . ." Emma shook her head then glanced Ruth's way as the child went to the store's huge picture window and looked inside, flattening her palms onto the plate glass. "Of course, one lesson won't fix it, but it's a start. If I keep doing it, well, I may not trust her around a street on her own for a long time, but maybe I won't have to keep a death grip on her, either. Like you said, consistency."

"And talking to her about it." He liked giving Emma advice because he really hoped it helped and because it made him feel better to think that after she had left Gall Rive and gone back to the world of fancy clothes and jewelry that something of him would go with her.

He headed for Ray Bob's, swung open the front door and held it for her. "I'm not a parent, of course, but what I've learned about people is that if they understand *why* they need to do something a certain way, they're much more likely to do it that way from then on."

"Finding the why, that's the toughie sometimes." She stopped on the sidewalk, glanced back at her daughter then met his gaze again.

He got the impression she wasn't talking about helping Ruth navigate through the world so much as finding her own way through whatever issue had her feeling so adrift.

"What were you thinking, Em?" Claire's voice rang harsh and agitated, even carried from across the street and down a ways. Dressed as if she had been expecting to spend the day in business meetings, Emma's older sister came marching up the other side of the street from the direction of the new city building. "That you brought Aunt Sammie into town the day after they let her out of the hospital is bad enough. But you leaving her on her own to wander the grocery store all by herself?"

"All by herself? She's only in a place where people have known her all her life," Emma called back, not showing one sign of letting her sister browbeat her on this issue.

"I know! And no less than three of those people have made phone calls to me already telling me that she shouldn't be out on her own like that and suggesting that maybe I was falling down on the job of taking care of her. That isn't like me and *you* know it." Claire wanted to emphasize that tidbit so strongly that she actually stopped where she was and jabbed her finger in the air to drive home the point.

Fascinated, Hank leaned over to ask Emma for a little clarification. "If she's so embarrassed by all this, why didn't she call you and tell you in private instead of shouting it to you from all the way over there?"

"It's like you said. People have to know the why before anything really sinks in." Emma crossed her arms over her Gator T-shirt. "So Claire is letting the whole town know why Aunt Sammie is alone and more to the point *who* is to blame for it."

Across the street and down a ways a tall thin man and a short plump lady, each carrying a brown paper bag from the Good Neighbor Grocery, flagged Claire down to have a word with her. Her gaze shot arrows of aggravation right at Emma.

"Anyway, to bring all this around to the pond . . ." Emma said as she headed back to the spot where Ruth had planted herself.

189

"Is that where all this was headed?" he marveled as he enjoyed watching Emma play up ignoring her obviously irritated older sis.

"Seems like that's where everything in my life is headed these days — a stagnant pool." She took the little girl gently by the arm. "Anyway, when Sammie Jo got home last night the first place Ruth wanted to take her was to the fence, which was just her way of getting close to the pond and that heron."

"Maybe she wanted to show your aunt my superior craftsmanship." Hank hooked his thumbs in his belt loops and puffed up his chest for effect.

"Right. Then why did she spend the whole ride back from Port Elaine unwrapping every piece of gum in Aunt Sammie's purse and making these?" She reached into the pocket of the child's oversize overalls and pulled out a cluster of small paper cranes. In one fluid motion she snatched him by the wrist, flipped over his hand and rained the delicate origami pieces down into it. "Ruth doesn't know what death is, so she doesn't get *why* the pond could be dangerous. When you can't change a child's behavior sometimes you have to change the environment around that child, to keep her safe."

"But maybe sometimes the way to shape a kid's environment is to allow them to take control of that environment by making their own choices. Maybe all that takes is for that child to be told by someone they trust — someone who isn't her mom — *not* to do something, to make an impression." He handed the folded paper bits back to Emma, all except one that clung to his palm. That one he tucked into his own pocket as a memento of this time, this special little girl and Emma. "Ruthie, you remember why I said you shouldn't play around the pond?"

"Bugs." She squashed her nose against the glass, which gave her words a smooshy-but-nasal quality.

The conversation across the street ended and Claire drew close enough that Hank could hear the quick clip of her high heels on the pavement picking up speed.

"You want to get a bug?" He reached down to lift the small girl up so that they could speak face-to-face, and so he could whisk her off to the chaotic distraction of Ray Bob's if Emma and Claire got into an argument.

"Just the kind you keep in jars." Ruth held her hands up as though she had an invisible Mason jar in them.

Claire spoke for a moment with someone

going into the grocery store. Hank had no idea what she was saying but she shook her head, then nodded it, then shook it again.

He moved a few steps to the door and opened it, finishing up his discussion with the child in his arms. "So, you going to go into the pond?"

"Nope. Only go into the base-a-ment." Ruth said.

"That's only if there's a bad storm brewing," Emma reminded her.

Hank glanced at Claire, who had finally made her way to the curb directly across from them. He muttered to Emma out of the corner of his mouth, "Bet you wish ole Ray Bob had a base-a-ment in this place right now. Hurricane Claire is headed your way."

"Let her blow all the hot air she wants." Emma laughed and puffed a stray lock of hair out of her face. "I haven't done anything wro—"

"Aunt Claire!" Ruth yelled so loud it actually made it hard for Hank to hang on to her. "You gotta cross at the corner! It's the laws!"

Claire glowered but she complied.

Hank looked at Emma. "That buys us just enough time to —"

"Y'all coming inside or not?" Ray Bob

grabbed the door from Hank's hand, bent down to wedge a rubber doorstop under it then gave it a jiggle to make sure he'd gotten it securely propped open. "Hey, there, little lady, used up all them supplies already?"

Claire made her way across the street and headed their way.

The sun ducked behind a cloud.

"Go on inside. Save yourselves," Emma joked. "Like we were saying, some things you learn *not* to do by knowing why not to do them, other things you don't do because you trust the person who told you not to do them. But sometimes there are things that you don't really learn not to do until you've done them and find out for yourself what a bad idea it was."

"I'm going to remember you said that." Hank put a hand on her shoulder. "I'm not sure what you said or what it meant but I am definitely going to remember you said it."

Ray Bob ushered Hank and Ruth in as he stepped outside. "You know, Emma, had a used item come in just yesterday made me think of you and your pretty little girl here."

"Pink Bike!" Ruth called out as Hank settled her down on the dingy floor of Leverett's All Goods.

"Better!" Ray Bob slapped his hands together. "You stay right here and I'll go get it and show it to your mama. Y'all are gonna love this, I gar-on-tee."

Love was not exactly the watchword out on the sidewalk. The two sisters' voices dipped and rose, bantered and bickered like birds squabbling over the same nesting ground.

"Aunt Sammie is just fine," Emma said as if she were issuing a news bulletin, just the facts, to her sister. "As a nurse I know that this kind of thing happens a lot trying to get the meds just right."

"I'm not upset about Aunt Sammie. I understand better than anyone you couldn't keep her at home if home wasn't where she wanted to be. I'm just saying that you were the one in charge of her this morning and you should have gone into the store with her so everyone would know someone had an eye on her. Instead you came flitting over here to flirt with —"

"Flitting? I have never flitted in my life, and as for flirting with Hank?"

"It's exactly what you need!" The front bicycle tire poked out the door first, thumping over the threshold. From inside the store Ray Bob grunted, the front of the bike bumped along onto the sidewalk but instead of a second tire following it, there was more bicycle.

"It's green," Ruth protested as if that were the only objectionable thing about the slightly off-kilter monstrosity.

"Oh, no." Hank cringed at the all-too-familiar pea green, twin-basket tandem terror. Emma, on the other hand?

"I love it!" The argument with her sister all but forgotten, Emma made her way to the door and began tugging to help Ray Bob lug the thing Hank had once wished would never see the light of day again out onto the sidewalk. The sun glinting off the double set of chrome handlebars hardly shone brighter than the smile Emma beamed at Ruth, then Claire, then Hank himself as she announced, "It's the answer to the whole Ruth-wanting-to-go-for-a-ride problem."

"No, this is its very own set of problems." Hank held up his hands. "I'm telling you, Emma, steer clear of it."

"I have to side with Hank on this one, Emma. Getting Ruth a bike and teaching her to ride was the first step in giving her some independence. If she has to ride with you . . ." Claire didn't finish the sentence, which was probably wise because Emma looked like no matter what her sister said she was going to take it badly.

"I don't want to ride . . . I want to fly!" Ruth stretched up as high as she could, her hands waving.

"Good point, Ruth. Trust me, nobody is going to go flying on this thing . . . unless it's flying off a cliff because the piece of junk went swerving out of control." Hank hooked his hands over the middle bar and tried to push the thing back inside. "Put this back into whatever forbidden caves of forgotten junk you dragged it from, Ray Bob."

"Oh, quit being such a baby." The stocky older man smacked Hank's cat-clawed hands with a big red reflector that had fallen off the back fender. "I seem to recall you did all right riding this thing in the Founder's Day parade last year. Big hit."

"Yeah, when me and Mrs. Mendlebright took a hard left straight into the corn-dog-and-cotton-candy vendor that was certainly a bi-i-ig hit." He made a bold gesture like a crash and explosion for Emma's benefit but he shot Claire, who had talked him into riding the bike in the parade as his doing his bit for community service, a cold glare. "I still have the nightmares to prove it."

"Mrs. Mendlebright? Our old music teacher?" Emma walked the length of the bicycle-built-for-trouble, touching it here, patting it there.

"The same. And don't let that gray hair fool you, when she decides her half of a bike is going in one direction the other half of the bike better be prepared to make that trip with her." Hank let go of the bike, not because he was giving up on getting it back where it belonged but because he needed to regroup in order to get a good grip again. He mashed his maimed palms together to try to wipe off some of the grime from Ray Bob's store that already covered the handlebars. "What I'm trying to tell you, Emma, is —"

"You know how to ride one of these!" She beamed a smile at him. "That's perfect. You can teach me then I can teach Ruth."

"You can teach me?" Ruth eyed her mother suspiciously.

"I can't wait to teach you, sweetie." Emma grabbed the handlebars and ducked down low. "Zooom. Zooom. We'll be flying together in no time."

"No time," Ruth echoed, doing a little spin down the sidewalk.

Emma stood up straight and wiped the grit from the bike off of her hands onto her old jeans. "But first Hank has to teach *me* how to make this bike go."

"Emma, it's not that easy." He let go of that bike for just a few seconds and seemed to have totally lost control of the whole situation. Hank wondered if there was a larger lesson for dealing with Emma in that but he didn't have time to contemplate it. "I'm trying to tell you, you can't just hop on one of these and ride away into the sunset."

"Sunset? Hank, I don't want to take a cross-country trip on the thing." Emma held both hands up. "It just seems like a terrific and totally safe way to introduce Ruth to bicycle riding."

"Emma, I am trying to tell you, this is neither a terrific nor totally safe way to ride a bike."

She dug into her jeans pocket and pulled out a slender wallet. As she dragged it out the diamond bracelet she had been wearing that first day came with it. So did some of the tiny paper cranes Ruth had made on the trip home with Sammie Jo. Emma poked the bauble back in as if it meant nothing to her, but made sure to collect all the small bits of folded paper and tucked them carefully away.

Hank thought of the crane he'd kept for himself and realized that no matter what happened from this point on, he and Emma would always have this unseen but unbreakable bond between them — they both wanted the best life possible for Ruth.

"Okay, Ray Bob, let's talk business. I don't want to buy this big old bike, but I wouldn't be opposed to renting it for a few days." Emma raised her wallet. "How much?"

"Take it for a day. Try it out." Ray Bob rolled the bike toward Emma.

"You won't even need it for a minute." Hank rolled the bike right back at the store-keeper.

"Freebies, Ray Bob?" Emma didn't seem to have heard a word Hank said.

"Anything for one of my Samantha Jo-lene's girls." Ray Bob rolled the bike to Emma again.

"Remember what I said about reminding you that you said some things have to be learned the hard way?" Hank put his foot out to stop the bike on the sidewalk. It fell toward him, banging against his leg and gouging him in the gut with the handlebar grip. "Learning to ride *this* bike, with someone else in tow on the backseat, is the very definition of 'the hard way' . . . times two."

"She'll take it." Claire pushed her way between Ray Bob and Emma. She seized the handlebars and began to wheel the clunky bike toward Hank's truck. "At least for one day. That's all it's going to take."

"Take for what?" Hank wanted to know,

199

not liking the sound of that at all.

The gentle breeze that had been ruffling the flag shifted, picked up velocity.

"You'll want food." Claire had to struggle slightly to keep the bike moving as a gust of wind hit her sideways.

"Take it for what? Food for *what?*" Hank refused to budge an inch until he got an answer.

He had allowed Sammie Jo and Claire Newberry to run roughshod over him for years, because he liked them, they were as close to a decent family as he'd ever known. But now, with Emma here, even if only for a while, and the feelings her presence and her daughter had reawakened in him, Hank felt he had to protect them, put their needs ahead of even the other Newberrys. He wouldn't be a party to Claire trying to get revenge on Emma by sending her out for a miserable experience.

"Mommy's gonna teach me too much." Ruth yelled at passersby coming out of the grocery store.

Especially when she had dragged Ruth into this by ramping up the child's expectations.

"Claire?" Hank stuffed his hands into his pockets and waited.

"Hey, you and Emma are the ones who

are all about who controls what and how do you teach Ruth or if you even think she can learn something. But in the end, all kids, even special-needs kids, learn what they live and what they see the people they care about live." She wrestled the tandem bike to the curb and settled it to rest against the fender of Hank's truck. "So I'm telling you two to go out there and live a little. If you can't do it for yourselves, you should at least do it for Ruth."

"Aaa-ooo!" Ruth howled the way her great-aunt Sammie Jo had taught her. "Go fly, Mommy. Just look out for the boo-gun-veel-yas!"

CHAPTER ELEVEN

"So, did you pack this lunch, Ruth?" Hank expected a bit more heft when he lifted the green-and-yellow wicker picnic basket by its handle and it went swinging. He'd wrestled the cumbersome tandem bike into the back of his truck and tried to keep up with Emma's driving. That had him physically weary but wired and his nerves on edge. At least that's what he had decided to credit for the sense of being slightly off balance as he stood in the drive of the bird sanctuary getting ready to spend the next few hours alone with Emma.

Alone with Emma. It had been so long since they had actually, really been alone together. Hank wasn't quite sure how it would go. He thought of the near kiss. He thought of holding her in his arms the day she'd arrived. He thought of all the years of brokenheartedness between them, all the mistakes, all the mistrust.

The shifting wind whistled through the broken iron gates and sent them creaking.

There had been talk that Claire and Ruth would follow in the car behind them as they tried to master the art of tandem bike riding, but everyone — everyone over four feet tall, that is — agreed that it would only agitate Ruth to have to watch her mom and Hank on the bicycle, with her unable to participate. So the child had been recruited to help with the lunch prep.

Hank leaned down to take Emma's daughter into his confidence. "Let me guess — pretend fried pink chicken and pretend pink potato salad."

Ruth covered her mouth with both hands and giggled. "Pink chickens, that's silly."

"This all just came together so quickly there wasn't time to cook anything." Emma went breezing by, lifted the basket from his hands and attached it with a bungee cord to the rack over the back fender. "So she kept it light. Unassembled."

"Unassembled?" Hank made a face sure to delight Ruth's already near-giddy mood. "You realize you promised me lunch, not inexpensive Swedish furniture, right?"

Emma gave the bungee a tweak that made it go *sproing*. "Fruit, some local cheese, bread and two bottles of sparkling —"

"French wine?" he asked.

"Water." Emma fit the long plastic bottles into the baskets on either side of the back wheel. "You didn't really think I'd bring wine, did you? After all, I'm driving."

"You're driving? You're the one who's never been on a tandem before but suddenly you're going to drive?" Claire clucked her tongue then shifted her gaze pointedly toward Ruth. She might as well have flashed a giant neon sign that said Your Daughter is Watching, Choose Your Words and Actions Wisely.

"I think it might be better if you let me be the captain." Hank moved to the head of the bike.

"Captain?" Emma did not readily relinquish the front position. She smiled a bit too brightly at him and said through her teeth, "Don't you mean *Doctor* Captain?"

"I like that, but no need for formalities." He smiled back not at all confident that Ruth was buying their "we're just having fun not vying for who takes charge of this potential fiasco" act. "*Captain* is the proper term for the person in front on a tandem bike."

"Then call me Captain Newberry. I like formalities, especially ones where I get a title." She took the lead handlebars and swung her leg over so that both feet rested on either side ready for her to hop up onto the front bike seat.

She looked like the model for a piece of old-fashioned advertising, wholesome, full of life and fun. The wind picked up her hair and blew it off her shoulders. Her cheeks flushed with healthy color but it was her lips that he could not take his eyes off. Time and again since Emma's return to Gall Rive he had reminded himself that she was not here to stay, that she had come here running from something that she still kept secreted away in her heart, that whatever they had once shared was history. All that meant that what he had told himself the first moment he'd laid eyes on her still held true. Emma Newberry was trouble.

But Hank had never been a man to shy away from trouble. He took the second position. "Lead the way, my captain."

"Okay." She tossed him a sincere smile then stood with her feet on the ground and her hands on the grips, staring at the pedals for a moment. A deep breath. She squared her shoulders.

"You can do it." Claire put her hand on Ruth's back and directed the child back toward the house. "Just have fun."

The sun ducked behind the clouds again,

as it had been doing off and on all day.

"If we have any problems we'll just call you to come and rescue us." Emma pulled her phone from her pocket and flashed it.

"Uh, if we have any problems we'll just have to deal with them." Hank swung his leg over the bike and tried out the handlebars in front of him. "Cell-phone reception is spotty at best on anything between the end of this driveway and the highway."

"And if you have to walk all the way from wherever you need rescuing to the end of the drive to make that call, you might as well make the rest of the trip up to the house and tell us in person." Sammie Jo laughed and motioned for the others to follow her up the drive.

"Funny!" Emma's smile never failed as she waved and waved and waved as her family retreated. "We'll be fine. By the time we get back we'll be flying, Ruth."

Ruth threw her arms out to her sides and charged up the rise in the drive.

"Aren't we going to go?" Hank prompted.

"As soon as they are over the hill and can't see us." Emma waved then waved again then . . . "Okay." She exhaled. "Show me how to do this, Hank."

"I can't show you from behind you. For you to see what I'm doing you need to be where I am."

She nailed him with a skeptical glare over her shoulder. "Did you give Mrs. Mendlebright this much trouble?"

"Mrs. Mendlebright let me captain the bike."

"And tell me again how that ended?" She mimicked his earlier pantomime of crashing, explosion, even added some wild finger wriggles he supposed indicated flames.

"Point taken." He laughed. "Don't let it be said I am a man who is unwilling to learn from his mistakes. Here's how we do this."

Ten minutes later they were gritting their teeth as the tires seemed to find every rock and dip and rut in the old dirt road.

"Can't . . . you . . . steer around . . . some of . . . this?" Emma called out to him from the stoker's seat.

"You want to be up here?" he called back to her.

"Are you kidding? I can't see how to do this from up there. You aren't the only one who can learn from your mistakes. In fact, I'm learning quite a lot from your . . ."

He should not have looked back at her then.

He should not have let his thoughts wander to how smart she was. How funny. How amazing she looked in her jeans and T-shirt with the wind in her hair and the weight of the world lifted off her shoulders for just this short span of time.

He should have remembered Mrs. Mendlebright and the corn-dog stand.

"No-oo!" She shut her eyes.

Hank whipped his head around in time to see they were headed off the edge of a curve in the road. He fought for control of the bike as he called out, "Ease onto the brakes the exact same time I do. On three."

"On three what?" she called out.

"Open your eyes. And brake with me. One. Two." He kept his tone steady. He couldn't manage the same for the bike.

"Oh, that kind of 'on three,'" she said and as she said the word *three,* she stomped on the brake.

The whole bike jerked.

Hank hit his brakes but it was too late, he no longer had control over the path the bike was going to take for the next few seconds. The one thing he could do was minimize any injury for Emma.

The tires went sliding into the ditch alongside the road. Hank stuck his leg out, literally digging in his heel. It sank into the soft earth.

A thump.

A bump.

The bike was on its side. Hank was underneath it.

Emma was on top of both.

He met her gaze and softly groaned out, "Three."

The whole world went quiet except for the leaves rustling in the wind.

Emma busted out laughing first.

Hank joined in.

They managed to get the bike off Hank and both of them up to the top of the ditch.

"You okay?" he asked as he massaged his neck and shoulder where he'd taken the brunt of the fall. He worked his leg to make sure he hadn't sprained his ankle or blown out his knee.

"Just a few grass stains." She brushed off her clothes. "And . . . oh . . . I tore my jeans."

She poked her fingers through the gash above her knees and waved to him through it.

"Wear it as a badge of honor." He stretched and took a minute to look around them. "At least we had the good sense to crash in a nice shady spot. Picnic?"

They spent about a half hour enjoying the simple meal of cheese and fruit. It wasn't as if Hank hadn't been to great restaurants or eaten wonderful meals but this one stood out above the rest because he was sharing it with Emma. He kept that thought to himself though. He didn't need to hear about the wonderful places that Emma was accustomed to going with the mysterious doctor in her life.

"Looks like clouds are really getting ugly. We've had a lot of pop-up storms this summer. I think one of them might have been what blew your great blue heron off course."

"Poor thing." She repacked the picnic basket slowly. "You really think it's best to just leave him be?"

"I do. That's God's business, Emma, not yours. When you try to force a situation where something wild is involved, you can end up doing more damage than you do helping."

"Maybe you wouldn't be so sure of that if you had your own broken bird that you were afraid would never really fly." She looked off into the distance.

He followed her line of vision. A quick flash of lightning illuminated the graying sky. "Let's head back. We don't want to give anyone reason to talk by staying out too long."

"That sounds more like the old Hank talking."

"I *am* the old Hank." He grunted as he

pushed up to his feet. "Emphasis on the old."

"Ha! You are *not* old." She looked at him from the corners of her eyes.

Was she flirting with him? He thought of his own speech about forcing a situation doing more damage than good. He just gave her a nod and went to the bike and looked it over, trying to decide if they should even bother righting it and trying to ride it or consider walking the mile or so back to the bird sanctuary, and coming back in his truck to pick the thing up. He decided to at least get the bicycle off the ground to look it over. He bent and grabbed the handlebars.

"Anyway, I can't imagine that guy riding a bicycle-built-for-two in a town parade, much less doing so much for Aunt Sammie or being so sweet and patient with Ruth." Emma was at his side on the slope of the ditch. She reached down for the second set of handlebars then looked up at him. "The Hank Corsaut I knew was so determined to prove himself to people here. He so wanted to be taken seriously. He cared so much about what other people thought of him. Looking back I wonder if he'd even figured out what to think of himself."

"That guy sounds like a real loser," he whispered, realizing that working together to raise the bike had put them only inches apart. "Why'd you ever agree to marry a guy like that?"

As they both pulled the bike up at once she said, "Because I knew that deep in his heart that guy was a good man. Kind, funny . . ."

"Don't forget devastatingly handsome." They got the bike up on its tires.

"Not half as handsome as he is right now." The second she realized what she'd actually said, she turned loose of the handlebars and put her hands to her face. "Oh! I didn't mean that the way it sounded."

"Really?" He caught the bike before it fell over. " 'Cause I liked the way it sounded."

"I didn't mean your looks. Not that you aren't . . . because you are. You definitely are." She stepped back and gestured more than was necessary as she tried to explain herself. "I was trying to say that I find this new you, the present-day you . . . Let's say I really appreciate your maturity."

"Ouch! Was that meant to sting? Because it did. A little." He held his thumb and forefinger apart a fraction of an inch to show how much. The bike slid to the ground between them again. "It's sort of like me telling you that after all this time it's good to see you still have your . . . great . . ."

She cocked her head. Thunder rumbled overhead. "Yes?"

"Personality," he concluded.

"Personality is an asset. So is maturity." She tipped her head and hooked her thumbs through her torn jeans as the Gall Rive Gator stared bug-eyed from her shirt. "Just try having an engaging intellectual conversation without a little of each."

Without having to support the bicycle the two of them were simply standing on the slope beside the road, a little off balance, a little too close for two people practicing maturity and claiming to value each other for their personalities should be.

"Emma?" Hank said her name softly.

"What?" she answered in kind.

He moved in closer to her, so close that the wind swept her hair out and it clung to his shirt. He put his hands on her shoulders. "What if I don't want to have an engaging intellectual conversation right now?"

She laid one hand along his cheek and rose up on her toes to put her face just beneath his. "Are you suggesting we should be shallow and immature?"

"Say that again," he murmured. "Just the last word. Slowly as possible this time."

"Imm-a-tur-r."

It put her lips in perfect kissing position.

Hank did not pause to think if what he did next was shallow or immature. He only knew that he had been wanting to do it since two days ago when she stood so close to him on the walkway that he could see the light in the depths of her pupils and the blush of heat beneath the warm, tanned glow of her cheeks.

He took her in his arms and pulled her close to him. In a minute, maybe two, she might push him away and tell him that they could never be more than friends. But as he drew in the scent of the earth, of the rain somewhere in the distance and of Emma, time suspended for him. There was no tomorrow, no yesterday, no long past or distant future each filled with their own brand of regrets. There was just now, this man, this woman, this kiss. Nothing else mattered.

After so many years of missing her, Emma was in his arms and no one could take that away from him.

"Emma! I can't believe I found you out here in the middle of nowhere. I had your aunt's address plugged into my GPS and —" A car door slammed. A tall man with golden hair and a tan to match stood just a few feet away. "What's going on here? Who

are you? And why are you kissing my fiancée?"

CHAPTER TWELVE

"Fiancée?" Hank leaned back, keeping both his hands on her shoulders. "I didn't know you had a fiancé."

"I don't." She curled her hand to fit over Hank's muscular arm even as she turned her upper body toward Ben and said, firmly, "I *don't* have a fiancé."

"You will as soon as you come to your senses and put on this ring." He slid a small blue velvet box out of the pocket of his pressed khaki pants and held it out to her. "I've already taken two days off this week because of this foolishness, Emma. Let's get this taken care of so we can get back to our real life."

"This *is* my real life." She sank her fingers into the soft fabric of Hank's shirt as if it might just be her lifeline to that life. "Or at least a part of it."

"The part that's in the past." Ben pushed the ring box toward her. "Leave it where it belongs, Emma, and give me your answer."

The man wasn't asking, he was telling her. It was as if it never occurred to him that she would say anything but yes to his proposal of marriage. Any other man might have taken the hint when the last time he'd asked the girl to marry him she'd jumped up from the table, run out of the restaurant and hadn't stopped running until she'd put nearly a thousand miles between them. Not Ben Weaver.

In some ways that was what made his offer even remotely worth contemplating. The man knew Emma didn't love him. He was okay with that. They had their work in common. They attended the same church. They had the same expectations in life about having a good home, healthy children and lives of service to others. Most of all he loved her and she needed a helpmate and coprovider for Ruth. With his connections, financial security and his penchant for never hearing *no* unless that was the answer he wanted to hear, he could do things for Ruth that Emma, who tended to get impulsively caught up in the moment, could only dream of. Given all that, it was hard for Emma not to believe as Ben did — that in time she would come to love him.

Many good marriages, Ben had argued,

had been based on less. When he laid it out for her it all made such good sense. But good sense did not seem nearly enough to make her stand before the Lord and pledge to love, honor and obey. If she had been willing to settle for a man who made good sense, she'd have married Hank all those years ago.

"Ben, I —"

"Ben? *Doctor* Ben?" Hank leaned forward, swinging his hand out to offer it in greeting to the other man. "Eat any good bugs lately?"

"Wh-what?"

"Ruth told him the story about you choosing a lobster from the tank at a restaurant, only she called it a big bug."

"I see." Ben eyed the other man with all the intensity he might use going over the results of a patient's MRI. His gaze moved slowly from Hank's dirt-smudged T-shirt to his open hand covered with tiny scratches, and the other one still on Emma's upper arm. Finally Ben gave a subtle nod and summed up "A funny guy."

"Hank Corsaut." Hank extended his hand again.

"Doctor Hank Corsaut," Emma said, not because she thought it meant so much to Hank that Ben know his title, but because she honestly wanted to show Hank the respect he deserved for all he had accomplished and all he did here in Gall Rive.

"Doctor Ben Weaver. Neonatology." Ben took a few hurried steps from the side of his sleek black convertible toward Hank standing beside the slightly-more-warped-than-when-they-started-out frame of the tandem bike. "So you're a doctor, as well? I suppose out here you're limited to family practice, mostly kid stuff."

"Oh, yeah, kids, calves, colts, puppies, even hamsters. I spend a lot of time helping Sammie Jo with her bird population, now and then someone brings in an injured possum or raccoon. I've treated a lovesick llama and a depressed tarantula and one Monday a month I get really brave and take on cats."

"Cats? You're . . . you're a vet?" Ben thrust his hand into Hank's and got in one firm shake before both men froze and looked down at their grasps.

"I believe this was intended for you, Emma." Hank flipped his palm up to reveal the blue velvet box that had formerly been in Ben's hand.

Her mind knew it meant nothing that Hank was standing before her holding out an engagement ring, but try telling that to her heart. It leaped and sent her thoughts careening more wildly than the misguided ride they had taken into the ditch not so long ago. It was all this marriage talk, she told herself. It was playing with her emotions. She just needed . . .

Ben snatched the ring box away, gave Hank a perturbed look, then took a moment to raise the lid and reveal the huge honking sparkler of a diamond engagement ring, which he held out in front of her. "Emma."

Emma held both hands up. Her shoes swishing in the grass sounded her retreat. "Ben, I — I'm afraid I haven't had time to . . . I told you last Thursday night that I needed more . . ."

"Clearly, you're confused," Ben said to her then aimed a heated glare at Hank. "Come with me and we can talk this through. I'd like to get moving before that storm moves in."

"Storm?" Emma lifted her head toward the dark clouds on the horizon and suddenly realized they had crept closer. And grown darker. Here and there lightning flashed against the angry sky.

"National Weather Service has issued a severe weather advisory." Ben followed her path, his arm out as if he intended to shepherd her physically, if need be, into his car. "You'd better come with me. For your own safety."

But it wasn't *her* safety that troubled Emma. "Oh, Hank, we'd better get back to the sanctuary. I've lived through hundreds of storms with Sammie Jo, she's terrible about trying to get things tied down outside before a storm and not making it inside before the rain and wind starts."

"Not to mention all the times she's told me about how much she enjoys sitting on the balcony watching nature's fireworks." Hank bent to pull the bike upright in one clean, quick movement. The seamless action emphasized the power of his shoulders and arms. When he turned just his head to scan the threatening sky, the wind whipped his hair every which way. He looked nothing like the dismissive "funny guy" that Ben had labeled him, particularly when he hoisted that bike off the ground and strode up the embankment to the road before setting it down again. There were some advantages to working with kids and calves and even llamas that a neonatal specialist simply did not benefit from.

Hank lowered the bicycle tires to the road then let the frame lean against his thighs as he turned to Emma and added, "Of course, you know Sammie Jo's not a storm chaser, so she's actually got her binoculars out watching the sky for birds in trouble."

"Balcony? Binoculars? Birds?" Ben shook his head. "This aunt of yours, Emma —"

"Is back at her house with Ruth." Emma took the back handlebars and swung her leg over to take the stoker position, relinquishing control to Hank in order to do what she needed to do to get to Ruth as quickly as possible. "Let's go!"

Hank didn't argue or try to tell her to calm down. He took the captain's position, ready to rush to Ruth's aid without question.

It made her heart swell. Confused? Yes, but not about this. When she had adopted Ruth all those years ago she had made a commitment to Ruth, to herself and to God that she would put that child's needs ahead of her own.

"Let's take my car." Ben's hand fit into the crook of her elbow. "It will be so much faster."

She met Ben's kind eyes. He was a good man, of course. She would not have gone to work for him if she hadn't thought that. Nor would she have ever even considered his proposal of marriage, based on his affection for her, all they had in common and all the things that he could provide for her and

222

Ruth. Emma squeezed the handlebar until the rubber grip burned against her palm.

Without her having to say a word to voice her conflict, Hank twisted his upper body around to face her and said, "Do what you need to do to give yourself some peace of mind."

She let go of the bike handle, threw her leg over the bar. "It's just that Ruth . . ."

"Ruth will be fine. I didn't mean to scare you with that balcony talk." Hank squeezed and released the hand brake a few times.

A subconscious message signaling that he wanted to stop her from going with Ben? Or just testing them out before he rode back to the sanctuary? Emma took a step toward him. He was probably right. Ruth *would* be fine. Even struggling with it, they could be back at the sanctuary by bicycle in ten, maybe fifteen minutes.

"Sammie Jo would never do anything she'd think would put that little girl in danger," Hank reminded her.

Emma lifted her chin to nod her agreement but Ben's cautionary tone made her freeze.

"Sounds to me that this Aunt Sammie of yours might just have vastly different ideas than you and I do of what constitutes danger." Ben tugged her toward the waiting convertible.

Emma lowered her head slowly, her shoulders slumped forward slightly. Once again Ben made perfect sense. Her heart wanted to go with Hank, but her head told her that Ben presented the best option for Ruth, and Ruth had to be her first priority.

"Why don't you ride back with us, Hank, and you can come get the bike in your truck later?" she suggested as she let Ben guide her to the sleek convertible.

"Because it's not my bike. I promised Ray Bob I'd take good care of it." He gave the tire a light kick then laughed and shook his head. "Least I can do is not leave it out in a storm to get blown around and sit out to rust."

"But —"

"Go," Hank mouthed. As Ben opened the passenger door and urged her to get in quickly, he called out, "But don't be surprised if when you get there Sammie has everything under control."

Emma paused, not sure if that thought should comfort her or scare her. "I'll be praying about her."

"Me, too." Hank gave a wave. "And for you, too. Don't worry."

The idea that Hank would be lifting her child up in prayer and cared about Emma's emotional state did comfort her. She slid into the seat, buckled up and took a deep breath.

Eyes shut she had just begun to formulate a quick prayer when Ben gunned the engine, extended his hand and pressed a button on the GPS mounted in his dash.

"Drive three hundred feet then turn left. Then turn left," came the mechanical female voice.

"What? It's telling me to turn around? Wait, that's for going home." He started pushing buttons. "Let me find the last address I fed into this thing."

"Ben, I *know* the way home."

"Not home, Emma, to that bird sanctuary."

"That sanctuary is my home, Ben." She couldn't believe she said it but she wasn't sure she wanted to take it back.

Hank took off on the bicycle. "Still have an open seat if you want it."

"We'll see you when you get there." Emma waved him on. "Ben, just leave that alone and pull onto the road. I'll give you directions. I think those clouds are getting worse."

The wind had picked up considerably, as well. A gust swept across the road, causing Hank to wobble on the bike. He kept pedaling whereas Ben couldn't seem to get going at all.

"Did you feel a raindrop?" He held his hand out. "Maybe I should put the top up."

"Just go!" Emma gestured with both hands.

Ben gave her a big smile. "Where was that decisive streak when I asked you to marry me?"

Emma didn't even try to answer, she just pointed to the road.

He cranked the wheel to get the car onto the road again.

"I don't know exactly how far down the road it is, but you'll want to go that way." She gestured in a way that she thought perfectly showed the long, nearly blind curve that Hank had suggested she took too fast. A fat, cool drop of water plopped into her open palm.

Ben let out a "humph," reached out to the GPS again and pushed here and there on the screen display. The voice returned with instructions to "drive point-eight miles then keep right."

Another drop.

Hank struggled with the bent bike up ahead.

"Maybe you should go a little faster, Ben."

"And maybe you should have been doing

more to slow things down, Emma." As soon as Ben spotted the other man he hit the gas pedal and asked Emma, "Just who is that guy and why was he kissing you?"

"He wasn't kissing me," she protested. "We were kissing each other. And he's . . ."

They passed Hank, who motioned for them to keep moving. "Tell Ruth to mix me up a batch of hot pink tea for when I show up soaking wet!"

The memory of finding Hank Corsaut having a tea party with Ruth her first day back made Emma's heart melt. She shifted in the seat to face the man who had told her a few days ago that it didn't matter if she loved him with all her heart, he loved her and wanted to take care of her and give Ruth the best of everything. That had been the part that tempted her. Giving Ruth what she needed most. A few days ago that had meant private schools, specialists, experimental therapy, financial security. After these past few days back in Gall Rive, spending time with Aunt Sammie, Claire, Ray Bob and Hank, Emma found herself wondering if all those things were really what her daughter most needed at all. She swung her gaze from Hank to Ben. "He's . . ."

Lightning split the sky followed by thunder so loud it practically knocked the breath right out of her. Memories and marriage dilemmas evaporated. She turned her attention to the sky in the direction of the bird sanctuary.

The booming resonance of the clouds clashing actually made the car's windows rattle. Emma felt the power of the storm overtaking them in her bones and the fear of what might be going on at the bird sanctuary in her heart. The wind whipped up, thrashing leaves from trees and tossing twigs in the air. That was their only warning before the rain began to pelt them, blown sideways by relentless, powerful gusts.

Ben threw his arm up to protect his eyes.

The car stopped. So did Emma's heart.

Ben opened his door and leaped out to release the latch to allow him to put the top up on the convertible.

"I can't wait for this." Emma climbed out, as well. She tried to push the car door shut again but the wind prevented it. She decided to leave it. She had to get to Ruth. Ducking her head she began to run, picking her way down into the drainage ditch that lined the old dirt road.

"Emma! What are you doing?" Ben got back into the car and hit the button for the electric car top. "Get back in here."

"I have to get to Ruth. If I cut across the fields I can get there a lot —" The sole of her borrowed old-style tennis shoe hit a patch of slick dirt.

She gasped. She couldn't find her footing. Her stomach lurched.

The rain came down in drenching sheets.

She felt as if she'd never stop slipping and then . . . she did. *Wham!* Right on her seat.

It jarred her through the length of her spine and neck, all the way to her back teeth, which she kept clenched together as she concluded "— faster."

"Emma, you okay?" A dark figure asked from the edge of the road above and behind her.

She turned and pushed her hair from her face, only then realizing her hands were covered with claylike slimy mud. "I have to help Ruth, Hank."

"Well, injuring yourself isn't the way to do it." He climbed down carefully, one hand hanging on to small trees and tall grass and the other extended toward her. "C'mon, let's get you back to the car."

Hank's hand fit into hers. It felt so good, as if she was in the care of someone who would always look out for her. And for Ruth.

"Get into the car." His voice barely carried above the whistle of the wind and the spattering of the rain. "We need to wait this out."

"Wait?" She plopped into the passenger-side seat.

Hank crouched on the ground using the open door and his own raised T-shirt as shelter from the downpour.

"You're the one who said Aunt Sammie watched storms from the balcony." She swung her head around seeking wiser counsel in Ben. "We can't wait."

"Have you forgotten how summer storms are around here?" Hank had to yell to be heard. "This will blow over in ten, maybe fifteen minutes, tops."

"Fifteen minutes is too long." She imagined her child cowering, confused, crying out for Emma, and Emma nowhere around to lend comfort. It made her heart hurt and her stomach clench. "Ruth is probably terrified without me."

"Emma, you have to let her . . ."

"Then we'll go to her." Ben stretched across the seat, across Emma, to catch the edge of window of the open door by two fingers. "Look, Dr. Corsaut, I don't know who you are, or what kind of claim you think you have on Emma, but she and I have a long-standing relationship based on mutual respect and a symbiotic partnership.

If she will let me, I will happily commit to spending the rest of my life taking care of her and of Ruth, so if you'll get out of my way, I plan on starting that commitment now."

Hank stood and let Ben yank the door shut.

Emma stared up at Hank, left dripping in the rain. "Aren't you going to let Hank get in —"

Ben put his foot to the gas. The engine growled but the convertible did not move.

Hank jumped back out of the way of the car's spinning wheels flinging mud behind them, splattering the bicycle-built-for-two from handlebars to picnic basket.

Emma groaned, her nerves frayed. She just wanted to get home. She just wanted to get back to Ruth.

"Drive point-six miles then keep right," the GPS instructed.

Ben reached to turn it off and knocked it from its perch instead. He lunged for it and in doing so his other hand dragged the steering wheel hard to the right. The car lurched.

"Don't worry about the GPS, Ben. Let's just get going."

More mud went flying, some of it hitting Hank.

"Be careful," Emma cautioned.

"What is it you want, Emma? To be careful or to not worry and just go for it? You have to decide."

Emma pressed her lips together. That just about summed up her whole life. She had been raised to embrace life with faith in God and joy in living. Those qualities made it impossible for her to settle for Hank's version of marriage without children and gave her the confidence to follow her dreams. But Ruth's disabilities and all the dangers of the world made Emma so afraid she had started to approach everything, from driving in the rain to falling in love, with the utmost caution, always looking for confirmation that everything would work out for the best before she even took a step.

She looked over her shoulder at Hank. Drenched and dirty, he stood in the road wiping off the bicycle seat with the hem of his T-shirt. The man had gone so far to try to help her.

Then she looked at Ben who had come so far to let her know he didn't want to lose her.

She just could not choose because these two were not her priority at this moment. They couldn't be. "What I want, Ben, is to get to Ruth."

"Fine." He stomped on the gas. The car sped forward, and following the direction of the steering wheel, dived nose first into the drainage ditch.

Emma flew face-first for the dash but the seat belt kept her from hitting her head.

Ben hit his cheek against the steering wheel.

Hank was at her window within seconds. "Are you both okay?"

Emma looked around. The air bags had not deployed but the front bumper of the car was wedged headlight deep in grass and dirt.

Lightning clashed on, slashing the sky all around them but most especially in the direction of the bird sanctuary.

The rain battered against the car in what sounded like hard little explosions.

Hank yelled to Ben to ease onto the brakes and turn the wheels as he tried to push the car free.

It rocked.

The wheels churned. They did not budge.

Hank came to the passenger door, opened it and said, "I think we're going to have to wait it out, then walk over to get my truck to pull you free."

Emma moved forward to give her onetime fiancé room to climb into the backseat behind her hoping-to-be future fiancé.

Hank settled in.

Ben shut off the engine.

Emma gazed off in the direction of Ruth and the sanctuary.

"Guess this gives us time for a little chat," Ben observed, in a flat humorless tone.

"Sounds good to me," Hank said, his eyes practically burning into the back of Emma's head.

Emma pushed her shoulders back and shut her eyes, her heart heavy, her fears running wild and her mind . . .

"Recalculating," chimed the GPS just seconds before Ben reached over and shut it off.

CHAPTER THIRTEEN

"What's the story with this guy?" Hank jabbed his finger at Dr. Ben Bug-eater only to find the man pointing right back at him.

"You still haven't told me about him." The other man didn't ask Emma so much as demand an explanation from her.

Emma didn't flinch. Or bristle. Or even take her eyes off the skyline out the mud- and rain-streaked windshield.

Kind of gave Hank the sense that she was used to getting orders from this guy with the fancy car and the big shiny diamond engagement ring in his pocket. And he couldn't help remembering the flashy diamond bracelet she had on that morning when she had showed up at her aunt's.

He looked at the woman he had kissed only a short time ago and those issues fell away. Her expression was grim. All the color drained from her cheeks. He could see the anxiety in her eyes, in the stiffness of her back, the tremble of her fingers as she put them to her sweet lips.

He put his hand on her shoulder. "Em?"

"I don't owe either of you an explanation for who I spend my time with," she snapped, looking from Hank to Ben and back. "Yes, Ben, I've worked in your office for more than a year now and we have gone out, but only five or six times. Your proposal came totally out of the blue for me."

"I hope that's not your way of saying no." He reached into his pocket, pulled out the ring box and sat it on the console between them. "Wait, let me rephrase that. I hope that's your way of saying you're still open to the idea."

Emma ignored the remark and the ring. "And, Hank, you and I parted paths a long time ago."

"Really?" Ben raised an eyebrow. "Because the way it looked when I drove up, you seem to both be on the same path."

Emma covered her eyes and shifted in the seat. "I don't need this right now."

"What do you need, Em?" Hank settled his hand on her tight shoulder, offering himself for whatever role she asked of him.

"A friend," she murmured.

"You got it." Hank leaned forward in the car so that his shoulder rested against the back of her seat. He clasped his hands between the front seats, blotting the engagement-ring box from his view.

"And someone to pray with me that Ruth and Sammie Jo are all right back at the sanctuary." She held her hand out to Hank.

He took it. It felt good to touch her, to do this much to comfort her. It felt even better to know she had asked him to be a part of her faith and her desire to lean on the Lord. He tried not to have any animosity when she did the same to Ben. If ever there was a time to set aside his questions and just stand with Emma in love and faith, this was it.

The car fell silent for a moment. Emma squeezed his hand, which had always been the Newberry family signal for "your turn to pray."

Hank took a deep breath, cleared his mind and heart and began. "Father, nothing is hidden from Your sight. Not Your children or their hearts, not their fears or their joys. Your eye is on the sparrow and we know we are just as dear to You. Please keep Your eye on our beloved little Ruth and Sammie Jo to see them through this storm safely. Give them your shelter, support them in their own abilities that they would be smart, not scared. And bring us soon to be united with them."

"Amen," Ben hurried to add.

Emma hesitated a moment then whispered, "Amen."

She turned loose of Ben's hand first.

Hank shouldn't have taken any pride in that or read it as a sign of which of the two of them she had the strongest connection to.

She drew both her hands up to her chest and kept her head bowed for a moment. It all seemed to be coming down on her at once, like the torrents of rain pounding down onto the ground, the car, bending the branches of the trees.

Hank wished he knew what to say or do to ease her anxiety but he knew he couldn't. She was a mother separated from her child — he had to respect her response to that situation.

One of the branches above them creaked, then a loud crack. It fell a few feet away, making Emma jump.

Hank laid his hand her shoulder. He didn't say a word, just let her know he was there.

"I hope that didn't scratch my car," Ben muttered. When he looked over at Emma her expression made him clear his throat and hurry to add, "Just being practical. It's who I am, Emma. It's one of the things people rely on me for, my pragmatism makes me a better doctor."

"Yes, but I have to ask myself, will it make you a better daddy?" she asked softly.

"For a child like Ruth?" He took Emma's hand and gave it a squeeze. "I believe it's what she needs in a father, a steady hand, an advocate."

Hank wanted to butt in and give his opinion about *that,* except some of what the man said was pretty close to the kinds of things he'd been telling Emma these past few days. On one hand, it really irked him to find this guy wasn't a total jerk. On the other, he had to be grateful that if Emma ended up with him . . . at least he wasn't a total jerk.

"I guess that's something to take into account . . . but not right now." Emma leaned forward to peer out the windshield.

The rain had begun to let up. The wind calmed. They sat there listening for signs that a new onslaught might be about to unleash itself on them. For a minute, maybe two they waited and watched the sun break through the clouds and beam down like spotlights on the field that Emma had planned to slog through to get to her daughter.

"Now it's time to go to Ruth," she said

239

more in an exhaled sigh than an actual announcement. In a flurry of movement she plucked a pen from the sun visor on her side of the car, gathered all her windblown hair into one hand, gave it a twist then used the pen to sort of stab it into place up off her neck.

"Nice," Hank murmured, talking as much about the no-nonsense skill of it all as he was about how good she looked, all casual but in command.

"Thank you." She gave him a nod. "From this point on, I am going to be captain, if you don't mind."

Hank smiled.

"Captain?" Ben frowned. "What . . . is that some kind of joke or . . . ?"

"Oh, believe me, when this girl decides she's ready to take control of a situation, she takes it seriously."

"I say we hike for it." Emma pointed straight ahead. "Then we get Hank's truck and come back for the car and bike. After we're sure everything is okay with Ruth and Aunt Sammie, of course."

Ben leaned forward to peer up through the windshield at the sky. "Don't you think we should wait out the rest of the rain?"

Emma already had the passenger-side door popped open. "If we start for home now, the rain will be stopped by the time we're halfway there."

"Makes no difference to me. I work outside in all kinds of weather." Hank gave the well-dressed neonatologist an overly strong-handed pat on the back. "Okay, Emma and I go get my truck —"

"Or just you, alone," Ben suggested.

"I'm going to get to Ruth." Emma got out of the car.

Hank worked his way to the door then got out, feeling as if he was unfolding himself in order to stand straight again.

"You sure you don't want to come with us?" Emma bent low to ask through the open door.

"I have plenty to keep me busy." The doctor waved his cell phone with every latest app and technological trinket.

"The sooner we get going . . ." Hank took Emma by the hand. It felt good, but not as good as shutting the door between Emma and her doctor friend.

She slid her hand into his and with a backward wave and a promise to be back soon, took her place by Hank's side.

He helped her up the other side of the ditch, over the tree roots and into the field. A stretch of mainly weeds, it didn't look much the worse for the sudden, violent storm. Hank thought that would bode well for the goings-on a mile or so up ahead at the bird sanctuary.

They walked briskly, Emma in short fast steps to match his long strides. He tried holding back but she raced ahead. Finally he just decided he'd keep up with her pace, whatever she wanted. And in doing that, he'd be able to find out something he had really been wanting to know ever since her secret doctor had showed up. "So, you're seriously thinking about marrying this . . . Ben?"

"I didn't say that."

"You didn't say no." He studied every bat of her eyelashes and twitch of her lips. "You came here to give yourself time and space to sort it out. That means you're considering it. Am I wrong?"

"You're not wrong." She picked her way around a boggy patch of dirt, and when they were walking side by side again, added, "But you're not exactly right, either."

Hank tipped his head up and aimed a heartfelt laugh skyward. "You're making me crazy, girl. You know that?"

They passed a tree with two larger and several smaller limbs blown down, the freshly jagged ends of the wood indicating it had just happened. Emma caught up one of the smallest branches and began to whack at the grass and weeds in front of her with it as she kept on walking.

Hank moved ahead and with a little bit of fancy footwork wound himself around so that he could walk backward and face her. "So, you're thinking of marrying the guy or not?"

"It's complicated. We'd get engaged now and plan a big elaborate wedding for next summer . . ."

Hank nodded, finding it easy to picture Emma as a summer bride.

"Then we'd spend that year finding the best neighborhood to live in . . ."

"I'm kinda partial to this one." Hank held his hands out to his sides.

"To find the best school for Ruth, the best therapies, whatever she needs, Ben is happy to provide it."

"So . . . you'd marry a man you don't love just hoping it would give Ruth an extra measure of security?"

She swished the tree limb lightly over the tops of the weeds. "According to Ben's scheme, I will have fallen desperately in love with him by the time we say our vows."

"Ben's scheme?" Maybe it was his frustration with the way this day had gone. Maybe it was his helplessness to argue against the romance of a man promising not just to woo her for a year but to also do anything for Ruth. Or maybe it just scalded his hide to have Emma in Gall Rive again and hear her talking about taking vows with another man. "What about *your* plans?"

"Hank . . ."

"What about making a spiritual connection and commitment? Have you two talked about that or is it all about what he can do for Ruth?" He stopped on a high spot in the field. On one side he could see the swath the two of them had blazed. It trailed back toward the place where Ben Weaver waited. On the other side he could see the uppermost eave of one of the attic dormers of the Gall Rive Migratory Bird Sanctuary. "Because I'm telling you that no matter what kind of special schools or therapists you find for Ruth, if love and respect and God are missing from her home, it won't really be a better place for her to grow and learn. What does this guy say about stuff like that?"

She stopped in front of him, tilted her head back to look at him even as she trudged on by him. "He says he loves me, Hank."

Hank watched Emma go by, undeterred in her singular purpose, to see to her daughter's safety. Of course the man loved her. What man wouldn't? "So he loves you. What about *me?*"

"I don't think he knows you well enough to love you, Hank. But if it's any consolation, he doesn't seem to actually hate you." She gave him a teasing look over her shoulder, giggled and kept on moving.

"I meant . . ." He sighed and took a few long strides to catch up to her again. "Emma . . . Emma?"

"The house is just over that hill and across the road." She pointed, her gaze fixed on the horizon.

He tried to stop her by taking her by one shoulder. "Emma, I'm trying to tell you something."

"And I'm trying to tell you something right back." Her gaze met his. A spray of raindrops flicked from the leaves of a nearby tree into her hair and onto her cheek. She wiped it away. "Ruth is my priority right now."

"I understand that," he said softly as she turned and walked away. "But what happens when Ruth grows up? What happens when she doesn't need you or want you hovering over her all the time? Kids turn into adults. Even kids with special needs. You can't stop it, Emma. You have to prepare Ruth *and yourself* for it."

The only way she showed that his words had hit their mark was a slowing of her pace for one step, two, maybe three, and then she gathered herself and pressed on.

Hank followed in silence but with every step that led her home, in every sweep of grass against his jeans, he heard the unspoken refrain that he wondered now if he'd ever get to say out loud to her again. "I love you, I love you, I love you, Emma Newberry."

Chapter Fourteen

With each step that brought her closer to home, Emma's footfalls went pounding through her body. Small limbs and leaves, fluffs of hanging moss from the live oak trees littered the front lawn, evidence that she had every reason to worry about the power of the swiftly passing storm. Before she got close enough to make herself heard by Ruth or Aunt Sammie, the main door on the second story swung open and Ruth came down the outside steps.

"We saw you from up high!" Ruth's feet hit the bottom of the steps and she began her uninhibitedly awkward way of running with her heels never touching the ground.

Emma did not cringe from anxiety or tell her to slow down in fear of how others might see her and judge her. Emma could not protect her daughter from other people's ignorance or fear, so she needed to help her child embrace her uniqueness. She saw that now in ways she never would have if she had never come home again.

Dropping to her knee, Emma folded her small, delicate child into her arms and drew her close. She shut her eyes long enough to say a prayer of thanks. When she opened them again and saw Aunt Sammie strolling down the steps, binoculars hanging around her neck, she had to ask, "Please tell me you did not take Ruth out on the balcony to watch for birds in trouble during that storm?"

Aunt Sammie opened her mouth wide to feign shock at the very suggestion.

"She wanted to," Ruth blurted out, letting go of Emma and twirling away with her arms out. When she came to a sudden stop, she looked up and over Emma's head and said, "I made her go into the base-a-ment like you told me."

"That's my girl." Hank stopped at Emma's side and gave the child a thumbs-up.

Ruth beamed with pride.

His girl. Just a few days ago she would have bitten Hank's head off just for using that innocent endearment. But then four days ago Ruth had belonged to Emma and Emma alone. Her fear-filled and fretful heart could not open to the idea that anyone else could love and care for and protect

Ruth the way she did. Emma still believed that no one could love her child the way a mother did, but no one could deny the ways Ruth had grown and come out of her shell around Sammie Jo, Claire and Hank.

This event, small as it might seem to others, was a watershed, a turning point in Ruth's life, and in Emma's, as well. Ruth had stepped out from Emma's sheltering wings — well, been allowed out from under them — and when faced with making a decision, had chosen wisely. After this Emma knew some part of her child would forever belong to this place, and to Aunt Sammie and even to Hank.

"She's not kidding. I headed for the balcony and she grabbed my hand and wouldn't let go until I got some food and went into the basement."

"Food, huh?" Hank sounded genuinely impressed.

"Yup, not pretend, neither." Ruth leaped into the air.

"As soon as the rain let up, we went up to the attic to look out the dormers to see if we could find you." Sammie Jo pointed to the open window that Hank was supposed to have fixed today. "You had me worried being outside on that bicycle in this weather."

Emma rose slowly from where she had greeted Ruth on the walkway. "I had *you* worried?"

"What mother doesn't worry about her child?" Sammie Jo pressed her hand to Emma's cheek, her usually loud and enthusiastic voice hoarse with emotion. "Did you think you were alone in that or that only mothers of children with special needs ever wondered if they'd given their children all the right tools to make the right choices in life?"

"Oh, Aunt Sammie." She wrapped her arms around her aunt's neck and kissed her cheek. "I had come to see myself so much as Ruth's mom that I'd forgotten that I'm still like a daughter to you, that I'm still Claire's sister and —"

"Somebody's fiancée?" Hank muttered to help her fill in the blank. He rubbed his hand back through his hair, sending water droplets here and there around him. Then he stuck two fingers into his front pocket and said, "I guess I'd better go get that car out of the ditch."

"Fiancé? You have a fiancé?" Sammie Jo looked from Emma to Hank seeking confirmation.

He held up his hands in a classic "I don't want to get involved" gesture.

Sammie Jo brushed aside a strand of hair that had fallen from Emma's makeshift bun. "Seems I was right to worry about you and your life choices, young lady."

"I haven't made any life choices." Emma pushed away, took a step, fixed her eyes on Ruth, who was wandering through the yard picking up sticks. "Ben Weaver is not my fiancé."

"Ben Weaver?" Sammie Jo scrunched up her face. "You mean your boss?"

"Only if I go back to Atlanta."

Her aunt grabbed her by the arm. "You're thinking of not going back?"

"This place has been good for Ruth, I can't deny it. I think she might thrive here. She's made some big leaps forward." The phone in her pocket vibrated to signal she was getting a text message. "Oh! Sorry, I should check this, it might be . . ." She glanced down. "Yes, it's Ben and he says . . . Claire was coming out to check on us, found him in the ditch and knew how to get the car out. They're checking it for damage before he drives it."

"Can we go to the balcony now, Aunt Sammie?" Ruth went gallumping past with a stick in each hand and started for the steps. "I gotta go see if that crane is waked up yet."

"Waked up?" Hank honed in on the same words that had sent a red flag up for Emma.

"When I saw it out the attic window it was sleeping." Ruth tipped her head to one side and laid her cheek against her hands, the signal Emma always used to tell her daughter it was time to lie down and be still.

A chill gripped Emma low in her stomach. She looked at Sammie Jo then Hank.

Both of them looked at her with grim expressions.

"Stay here for now, Ruth. Help Aunt Sammie make some lemonade for Doctor Ben. I've got to . . ." She couldn't finish that sentence.

She took off across the yard, needing to see for herself, hoping it was not too late to do something. The thought of that poor bird, injured, afraid, broken or worse clawed at her heart. She broke into a run, heading around the side of the house, across the back lawn and out to the pond.

"Emma, don't." Hank was on her heels.

She evaded his hand as he reached out to take her shoulder and hold her back. Guilt and fear, shame and regret rose in her chest. All she could think was that she had had it within her ability to protect that poor bird. She prayed it would still be true, that they would not arrive too late to help but deep down she knew she had taken her eyes off the task at hand and because of her . . .

She struggled to get the old picket-fence gate open and when it didn't swing smoothly she tugged it just open enough so that she could squeeze through the opening. The pond was still up ahead. She scanned from one side to the other, pleading with the Lord that the bird might lift its head and fix its quiet, wary gaze on her again. It did not happen.

Before she even reached the pond she had already begun to cry but when she finally laid eyes on the lifeless body of the great blue heron, Emma lost her last shred of composure. With her every breath the great, wrenching sobs from the deepest part of her being dredged up her darkest fears.

She had let her guard down. She had listened to the counsel of people who did not understand how much was at stake. She had failed this innocent creature who had only her to rely upon. It was her fault the heron was dead. All her fault.

If she could not protect a simple wild bird out of place in a bona fide bird sanctuary, how could she ever watch over Ruth and keep her child safe in the overwhelming, forbidding world?

A wayward remnant of wind swept over

the grasses around the pond, sending droplets of rainwater against her cheek, neck and arm.

Hank's hands settled down on her shoulders. "It's too late now."

"I know that. Don't you think I know that?" She batted one of his hands away. "But what about yesterday and the day before? I could have tried harder to get it to leave, to help it get to a place where it would have been safer."

"Where would that be, Em? If you had scared it away from here, could you be sure it wouldn't have gotten to a place where an animal might have attacked it? In shooing it off could you have guaranteed that it wouldn't have gotten sick or injured and lingered a long time suffering before it died?"

If that was meant to reassure her, it fell short by a mile. He seemed to be reminding her that no matter what she did, it could never be enough. So she'd just have to do more. She couldn't risk failing Ruth the way she had failed this poor bird.

"It's a harsh world. Life can be brutal. You can't live every minute terrified of what might happen. You have to be smart, not scared."

She wiped the tears from her face and

cleared her throat. "You know, Hank, I finally get what you mean by that and I couldn't agree more."

"You do?"

"If you know there is danger, you do whatever you can to guard against it harming you or the ones you love. Simple as that." Simple. Not pretty or romantic or even particularly deep. Emma sniffled and forced down a sob. Her direction now was simple. "I won't stand by and leave my little wounded bird of a child to the risks and hazards, the storms and random ravages of the world."

"Emma, Ruth is a human being, not a bird." Hank didn't just take her shoulders now, he turned her to face him, and when she wouldn't meet his gaze he bent to lower his face to make sure they had eye contact as he said, "Ruth is this great kid with so much potential. She has a natural curiosity that she needs to be taught how to manage, and her sense of humor . . . Emma, you can't wrap her up and keep her away from every danger without keeping her from living her life."

"Ben has offered me a way to do that, Hank. If I marry him he will provide security, a good home, good schools, and provide Ruth with two parents to look out for her. I have to at least give his offer more than just a reflex reaction. I have to give him a chance to show me that it can work. For Ruth's sake."

"What about love?"

"What about it?" Emma would never put her own romantic notions above the needs of her child.

"You can give Ruth all the right stuff, you can surround her with all the things that you think will keep the big scary world at bay, you can even provide her with two people to exercise guardianship over her 24/7 every day of the year for as long as they live but without love it will never be able to give her a family. She has that here."

Emma looked at the old house. There was some truth in what he said.

Hank sank his blunt fingertips into the soft flesh of her upper arms. He gave her a little jostle, as if trying to literally shake some sense into her, then whispered, "Stay, Emma."

She twisted her neck and shut her eyes so that she did not have to look at him or the house. "I can't."

"But this is your home."

She opened her eyes to stare at the silent, foreboding pond. "It wasn't, but it is again and I thank you for your role in that. No matter where I go, that won't change."

A car drove into the long drive and Emma took a deep breath. "That'll be Ben. I have to go." She turned and walked away.

"But . . . I love you, Emma."

Hank Corsaut loved her. If he had said those exact words, *But I love you, Emma,* all those years ago she didn't know if she'd have been able to have walked away. Then, it would have spoken of hope and possibilities. Then, Hank would have been the one she'd have given a second chance.

But now? Now was too late. Still, Emma knew that Hank's words would resonate with her all the way back to Atlanta.

CHAPTER FIFTEEN

"What d'ya think?" Emma stood behind her child, both of them dressed in their very best dresses, and ran her fingers through the little girl's fresh new short hairdo.

"Too-oo much!" Ruth tipped her head this way and that in the mirror.

"I guess that's better than not enough." Emma straightened away, trying not to dwell on the fact that even almost two weeks after they had spent those few days in Gall Rive, Ruth still spouted things she'd enjoyed saying there and always in the perfect Louisiana cadence of Sammie Jo, Claire and Ray Bob.

Ruth scampered off.

Emma's hand trailed off after her child. She wished she could bundle the little girl up and just sit and spend the evening . . . catching lightning bugs or blowing bubbles or playing with Earnest T and Otis. Emma checked her cell phone to see if she had any calls. Not that she expected any but Hank had said . . .

If you really loved someone, you'd call, right? she asked her image in the mirror. Of course, Emma hadn't exactly picked up the phone and called Hank, either. Oh, she'd picked up the phone plenty, she'd just never gotten the nerve to call the man and say . . . what?

She didn't have any business thinking about this, especially not now while waiting for Ben to show up for their first real date since she'd agreed to come back to Atlanta. They'd waited two weeks so she could resign and work out her notice. It just seemed the right way to handle it if they hoped to really change the direction of their relationship. Besides, it was only fair to the other people who worked in his office. The ones he didn't profess to love or shower with diamonds.

That reminded Emma of the bracelet he'd given her for her birthday, when he had first come up with his idea about them marrying. Where had she put that? "The last time I remember having it . . ."

An image of her standing on the sidewalk outside Ray Bob's. She could see Hank as clear as if he were standing here with her now. To sweep aside the memory of his nearness, she rushed to the bedroom closet to the pile of clothes she had slipped out of when she came back from Gall Rive. She snagged up the jeans and her fingers slid through the tear made when she and Hank crashed the tandem bike.

"You didn't come here to remember," she told herself through clenched teeth. She dipped her hand into one pocket then the next, and finally her fingertips brushed over the bracelet. She pulled it out but when she did a small shower of tiny gum-wrapper paper cranes came cascading out with it. She bent to pick one up and turned it this way and that.

"What do you wish for, Ruth?" In the child's entire life only Hank had asked Ruth that simple question.

Emma raised her head to listen to her daughter chattering to the mirror about hats and bougainvillea, pink tea and howling at the moon with her dog-friends. Emma couldn't help wondering if she had ever asked Ruth, "What do you wish for?" She didn't have to listen long to guess it would not be to live a life sequestered from the world with a bug-eating neonatologist as your benefactor.

Emma pushed her cluttered emotions to the side. She hadn't agreed to marry Ben, just to date him and see where it went. She got up and tried to fasten the bracelet around her wrist as she walked to the front room.

Ruth came twirling by, bumped into Emma, knocking the bracelet and the paper crane to the floor. She bent and picked up the crane. "Oooh. I can do this."

"You can do anything, sweetie," Emma said, stopping herself from following up with a string of qualifiers meant to spare the child from *over*wishing and getting hurt.

"Pretty but it can still be bended. It can get squashed." Ruth put the paper crane in her open palm. "My bird-friend got squashed, didn't it? It got flat and won't be when we go home again."

Emma blinked, dumbfounded. She wanted to ask her daughter how she had reached that conclusion but the doorbell ringing sent Ruth dancing off.

"Marriage proposal, take two." Ben stuck the blue velvet box through the doorway before Emma even got it open all the way.

"Is that for me?" Ruth leaped up in the air with her fingers wriggling.

Emma stood back to allow the man inside but she didn't have an issue making the boundaries clear to him. "I agreed to give our relationship a chance, Ben, I never said

I'd marry you. I've never been anything but honest with you about my feelings for you and my motives for seeing where all this might lead."

"Can't blame a guy for trying." He tucked the ring box away and stepped out of the doorway, almost running over Ruth. "Isn't she awfully dressed up for an evening at home with the babysitter?"

"Sitter?" Emma had spent all week back at work, and her evenings pouring over pamphlets for schools that took children with Ruth's disabilities. She had hardly had any time to spend with her child; she certainly wasn't going to go out and leave Ruth behind. "I didn't get a sitter. I thought she'd go with us."

Ruth put one finger up, tucked her chin down and looked up at him. "No bugs for me."

"It was lobster," Ben muttered, sidestepping around the determined child. "Emma, this was supposed to be a special night for us. Our first real date since . . ."

"Right." She understood completely the significance of this evening. She just wanted to be sure that Ben did, too. "This is the night we take the first steps that might end with us becoming a family. Ruth should be a part of that, don't you think?"

"Look, Emma, we'll bring her back something special from the restaurant but this night is for you and me." It wasn't a cruel or callous notion and yet there was something lurking beneath his mask of congeniality that made Emma uneasy.

"But there isn't just you and me, Ben. Ruth is —"

"Ruth is not really, um, ready —" he tipped his head toward the girl who was pressing her face against the mirror where they had just been admiring themselves "— to eat at a really nice restaurant."

"I know my manners." Ruth extended her pinkie finger, pretended to lift a teacup then let out a slurp so loud it made Ben wince.

He shot Emma a look and held his hand, palm up toward Ruth to offer her as evidence to support his claim.

She considered telling him that Hank had taught Ruth that. But did that really matter? "You're going to have to get used to the idea that as her parents, if it goes that way, we have to teach her by guiding her through new experiences."

And sometimes teach her by not guiding her, she thought, suddenly aware that her own actions had probably tipped Ruth off about the fate of the great blue heron.

"Isn't that what the private school is for?

The specialists?"

Her stomach knotted.

"You know, once we're married, if you want to quit working completely and . . . you know . . . devote your time trying to work with Ruth, I am fine with that. But tonight let's not, not . . ."

"Waste." Emma folded her arms and looked at the man as if she were seeing him for the first time.

"Yes, thank you, let's not waste another minute arguing over this."

"You were going to say I could quit work and *waste my time* working with Ruth." She knew this just as certainly as she knew that working with her daughter was anything but a waste. But she had been thinking that once she married Ben she would quit her job and spend her time watching over Ruth, protecting her, keeping her safe from the world. Wasn't that just a feel-good way of saying that Emma was going to waste her time, because as Hank had pointed out, she could never make the world safe enough to guarantee Ruth would always be okay.

"I didn't say that," he protested.

"You didn't have to," she said softly.

She had never thought in those terms before but suddenly, standing here trying to drag her poor child out on a date that even

Emma wasn't all that interested in being on, it hit her. Ben's lack of faith in Ruth's abilities might be emotionally worlds away from her overprotectiveness but the end result looked heartsickeningly the same. Ruth got the short end of the deal from Ben because he saw working with her as a waste, and from Emma because she thought working with her would only bring heartache and danger. How could she have not seen that?

"Don't put words in my mouth, Emma. Clearly I am not an overtly sentimental man. In order to do the kind of work I do, I have learned to be objective about things that other people become overwrought about. Ruth is your child and I hope the best for her, I genuinely do, but . . . well, look at her."

Ruth pitched and rolled and spun, her arms stuck straight out at her sides. "I'm flying."

Emma smiled. She got it. She got what Hank had been trying to tell her. Her heart filled with joy. "She's flying, Ben."

"She's not going anywhere."

"That's not . . ." Emma watched Ruth whirl around in place. She thought of the great blue heron that would not budge from its spot by the pond. It still pained her what had happened. Yet in that moment, seeing

Ruth as she was now after just a week in Gall Rive and hearing Ben describe her as going nowhere, her thoughts and fears at last caught up with her hopes, dreams and heart. Ruth was not like the heron. Ruth wanted to go out into the world; her little girl wanted to fly! Emma knew that feeling.

She would never deny that to Ruth. So what was the right thing to do? Just like the birds that came and went from the sanctuary year after year, the creatures that trusted God to see to their daily needs and never hesitated to lift their voices in His praise, Emma had to give her child wings.

"Ruth is going wherever her heart leads her, Ben. It may not be on the path that you would take. It may take her a long time to get there. She may have a lot of setbacks before she finds her way, but she will find it. And the best way I can teach her how is by my example."

"What are you saying, Emma?"

"Ben, you are a good man. But you are not the right man for me."

"Because of your daughter?"

"Because of my daughter. And my Aunt Sammie. And my sister and . . ."

"Hank Corsaut?"

"Hank Corsaut."

"In other words, you love him."

"In other words, I love . . . my family. And they love me. And Ruth. And where they are, that's where we belong."

She shut the door behind him, and leaned back against it. Could she really do this?

"Where did Doctor Ben go?"

"Out to eat bugs, for all I know." She laughed. "What really matters is what we're going to do."

"What are we going to do?"

"Fly, sweetie." She kissed the child's nose. "I hope you don't mind if we take the SUV to do it."

CHAPTER SIXTEEN

"I don't see why fixin' these old attic windows can't wait, Sammie Jo." Hank swiped a trickle of sweat away from the corner of his eyebrow. "They're not a danger to anyone now, unless you decide you want to climb out on the roof in a rainstorm to flag down passing pigeons."

"Pigeons?" Sammie Jo stopped wadding up old newspapers he had spread under each window frame as he stripped the old paint off them. She shook her head and laughed. "In Gall Rive?"

"Pigeons she laughs at. The idea of guiding birds in to land on her roof?" It was Hank's turn to shake his head. He refolded the square of fine-grain sandpaper in his hand and went at the windowsill again. "I still think these windows could have waited a while."

"No, sir. Now is the time. Feel that?" She raised her face and shut her eyes. The crosswinds created from all the windows flung open wide ruffled her graying hair. Her slender shoulders rose and fell with her purposeful, deep breaths. "Change is in the air. Won't be long now that autumn will come to the way-up-north sending the flocks in flurries back here to the place that generations of their kind have come to call their safe haven."

Hank swung his gaze to look out of each window and over the land, from the road that went to town to the old pond where he had last seen Emma almost two weeks ago. He wanted to tell Sammie Jo not to get her hopes up too much that the wayward birds, her own personal flock as it were, would return on the next cool breeze or for a long time to come. He'd looked for her himself for the first few days, thinking his profession of love would bring her to her senses and draw her back to him. When that didn't happen, he had to accept that spilling his heart out to her like that was probably one of the things that had pushed her away. She had run away from Gall Rive out of fear for Ruth's security but she had stayed away because of him.

It was the only conclusion he could come to. When a man tells a woman he loves her and she walks away, then what more is there for him to do? The ball is in her proverbial court.

Hank's arms and fingers, shoulders, back and neck ached from a full day of hard work prepping the windows, but it was the heaviness in his chest thinking of Emma and all he had lost when she left that made him lean against the wall and ease his breath between clenched teeth.

"That's why we got to get this place fixed up now. Once we get into the fall, there won't be time."

"Well, we made some progress today." He tossed aside the worn-thin sandpaper then leaned down to rub his fingertips over the smooth finish of the wooden windowsill. "All traces of its past are gone. It's ready for whatever comes next."

"Well, amen to that."

"I wasn't saying a prayer, Sammie Jo, I was making a comment about where we are right now."

"I was, too." She wadded the paper into a ball and made a high arcing throw into the trash can. "Home improvement or self-improvement, it's like the Good Book says, the old has got to pass away before the new can come."

"Amen to that, as well," Hank whispered as he watched the paper land easily in the can. "Okay, so the paint-scraping stage is done."

"Oh, hey! Speaking of scraping off the old paint, I gotta get cleaned up." Sammie Jo shook some of the paint chips off her shirt. "Ray Bob finally invited me in to dinner tonight."

" 'Bout time he made his move." Hank turned toward the open window and a small cloud of dust halfway between the house and the highway caught his eye. "You'd better get going. Looks like Ray Bob is already headed this way."

"He'd better not be!" She smooshed her hair against her head like a fine Southern belle patting a gloriously big bouffant into place, only Sammie Jo was working with a paint flake–speckled topknot that looked like a lopsided whale spout. "I still need to run a brush through my hair and freshen up."

Hank laughed at the understatement.

Sammie Jo continued gathering newspapers. "I'll sweep up in here before I have to get on with my predate prettification. You don't have to hang around and start painting. We can get to that tomorrow after church."

Hank started to protest that he might have plans tomorrow but it seemed silly. Even if

271

he did have plans, which he didn't, Sammie Jo would find a way to work around them in order to get the best use out of him possible. Another man might have resented that but Hank was finding some comfort in being around the only other people in town who came close to missing Emma and Ruth Newberry as much as he was.

"Fine," he muttered, wiping his paint- and dust-covered hands on his paint- and dust-covered T-shirt. He turned his face to the window again, thinking of how Emma had just come and gone from his life faster than the birds who touched down in this sanctuary while passing through in their migratory paths. This was not home for those birds and it was not home for —

The car on the dirt road kicked up a new puff of dust as the driver hit the long, tricky curve without slowing down. Hank gripped the window frame, his jaw tight and his throat so constricted he could hardly swallow. Could it be? "Company's coming, Sammie Jo."

"Is it a birder? Claire? Do you think it could be Ray Bob?"

"I think it could be . . ." Hank narrowed his eyes and followed the car's racing along the old road. He barely managed to raise his voice to a hoarse whisper as he finished,

"I think it could be trouble."

"One of us should go see what they want." Sammie Jo craned her neck to peer down the attic steps and grab a peek all the way through the stairwells to the first floor foyer.

"I wonder if she actually knows what she wants." Hank watched the silver SUV come gliding into the driveway of the old house and thump to a halt.

Without thinking, Hank jerked back from the window into the darkened shadows of the small attic. There was no reason to hope Emma had returned because of him. She wouldn't have come to the sanctuary expecting to find him here. In fact, she'd probably come back to announce her engagement, or maybe with her new husband in tow?

Better not to force an awkward and potentially hurtful meeting. He'd just hang back and wait it out until Emma realized what she'd walked into, however long that took.

He heard the car door open.

The front door of the house followed.

He braced himself to hear Emma's voice.

A confusion of dog nails clattering in the hardwood hallway made him wince. Instead of Emma his ears were treated to the joyous baying and barking of Otis and Earnest T turned loose on familiar arrivals.

"My dog-friends! Otis, Earnest T! Your Ruth is back!"

His dogs practically mowed the child over and she loved it. She giggled and squirmed and tried to pet them with both hands.

"Hello! Hello? Y'all? I'm sorry I didn't call first but . . . I wasn't sure . . ." Emma's voice carried all the way up from the first floor. "I'm home!"

"Home." Hank muttered the word she had spoken, trying not to read too much into it. He looked to Emma's great-aunt for some kind of clarification.

The older woman folded her arms, cocked her head and gave him a no-nonsense jerk of her head in Emma's direction. "Why are you still standing here? Go to her."

"She doesn't want to see —"

"Hank? I know you're here. I — I have something to tell you."

His heart hammered. He realized he was grinning and tried to look serious. He just couldn't do it. Emma had come home and she had something to tell him. Even if it was that she could never love him, just the idea that she had come back this time, that he had one more chance to talk to her, to see her again, made him take the attic steps at breakneck speed.

By the time he'd hit the second floor he

slowed down. When he reached the top of the staircase and grabbed the handrail, he was cool and collected. Outwardly. He took the first two steps and Emma came into sight.

One foot on the porch, the other in the foyer, she stood in the open door keeping an eye on Ruth in the yard. This time she did not return to Gall Rive flustered, exhausted and wearing diamonds and a little black dress. She tipped her head up and the sunlight splashed across her soft, unbound hair, the pair of jeans she'd had on the day she'd left, complete with torn knee from the biking accident, and a Gall Rive High T-shirt.

Hank thought he'd never seen her more beautiful.

"Hi," she whispered. "I, uh, I was in the neighborhood and . . ."

"I was just —" he pointed over his shoulder toward the attic "— fixing up your aunt's attic windows."

"Oh, good. Good." She gave a look out the door, pressed her lips together then called out into the yard, "Ruth, you are in charge of Earnest T and Otis. You keep them right there in the front yard, do you hear me?"

"Hear that, guys? *I'm* in charge" came

Ruth's reply.

Emma hesitated only a second more before she stepped inside and let the door fall shut. She came to the end of the stairway, placed her hand on the finial and rested one foot on the bottom step. "I'm glad you're taking care of those windows because Ruth and I are planning on sticking around awhile this time. It's the smart thing to do and you know what I always say — better to be smart than . . . Oh, who am I kidding?"

Her hand dropped. She squeezed her eyes shut and shook her head. "I've been anything but smart since the day I even considered Ben Weaver's proposal the first time."

"Hey, smart isn't always everything it's cracked up to be." Hank came down one step, then another. Not quite ready to go the distance without a little more confidence that he wasn't heading into another heartbreak. "I, personally, was very smart about the workings of the natural world when I told you to leave that heron alone. And I was over-the-top smart all those years ago when I looked at my own childhood and concluded that being a parent might be too much for me."

Outside Ruth squealed.

Otis gave a low woof.

Emma's back stiffened but she did not run to the front door to peer out and check on her child.

Her reserve was rewarded by the scuffle of a child's feet and dogs' paws on the porch and Ruth saying in a most grown-up tone, "Cool it, boys. Sit down and we can have pretend tea."

Hank smiled.

Emma smiled and sighed.

"Smart is only part of the picture." He came down the steps toward her, stopping halfway down the staircase. "The thing I didn't take into account all those years ago or just a couple of weeks ago was that smart is only a piece of the equation. The most important part is love."

"I thought that's what *you* taught me." She moved onto the first step, laid her hand on the rail.

"I do love you, Emma." He came down one more step but couldn't trust what was happening enough to make his way all the way to her. "And I love that pretty-great kid of yours."

"I hoped you'd still feel that way after I acted like such a . . . a . . . terrified child myself." She looked down. "But I took the chance and drove here unannounced be-cause I . . ." She looked at him at last, tears in her eyes. "I love you, Hank Corsaut."

"You do?" He started down the steps for her.

She swiftly closed the distance between them and threw her arms around him. "I do. I love you, Hank. I love you."

She kissed his cheek.

He took her in his arms and looked deep into her eyes. "I love you, too, Emma."

They shared a kiss that left no doubt in his mind that Emma Newberry loved him as he did her, with all her heart.

"Well, there's a scene that's been more than ten years in the making!" Sammie Jo appeared from her bedroom door on the second floor, dressed in a thick, long robe, with a towel wrapped around her head. She gave Hank a weary look, shook her head and clucked her tongue. "And you gave me grief over how slow Ray Bob and I have been in getting our romance back on track."

Hank opened his mouth to . . . what? It didn't matter. He chuckled. "There's no arguing with a Newberry woman who believes she's in the right."

Emma planted another kiss on his cheek, then another on his lips.

"And oh, how right this Newberry woman is for me," he murmured.

"It's here!" The front door flung open and

Ruth stood there, dogs at her heels. "Aunt Claire and that Ray Bob are here with it!"

"Ray Bob? Here? Oh, my!" Sammie Jo skedaddled up the steps and back into her room.

"They have a date." He couldn't stop looking at Emma. He ran his hand through her hair. "He wasn't supposed to show up for hours, though."

"I'm afraid that's my fault." Emma grabbed him by the hand and started leading him toward the front door. "C'mon. You're gonna love this."

"I already do," he whispered.

CHAPTER SEVENTEEN

Ruth went tripping out the door.

Emma laughed with joy at the sight then turned her eyes again to Hank's. Her heart soared.

"I'm so glad you came back." He tugged on her hand to pull her to him for one more kiss before they headed out the door. "I can't tell you how many times I almost took off for Atlanta after you but I'd made my feelings clear and you'd gone off. I thought trying to push it would only make problems for you. After all, I could never offer you all that Ben could."

"You've already given me so much more and I can prove that to you."

"All right." He leaned in to kiss her again.

She stole a quick peck then giggled and tugged on his hand. "Follow me."

"Anywhere."

She flung open the front door and brought him outside just in time to greet Claire and

Ray Bob as they pushed and pulled and wrangled the small pink bike that Ruth had fallen in love with out of the backseat of Claire's big old car.

"You're kidding me." Hank laughed out loud and clapped his hands. "Whose idea was that?"

"Mine!" Ruth said, clearly talking about the bike she had already begun to hug even before the wheels hit the ground.

"Actually, I believe it was your idea, Hank." Emma led him into the yard. "Your offer of a safety helmet and pads still stands, I presume."

"They're still in my truck behind the seat," he said.

"I found training wheels in Port Elaine." Claire moved from the bicycle to the trunk of her car. "This kid'll be flying before you know it, Em."

"Then I guess we'd better do our best to help her get prepared to do it right," Emma said.

"How you gonna do that there?" Ray Bob wondered.

Emma put her hand to Hank's cheek as she answered with all the things that she had learned these past few weeks. "By living the kind of lives that will teach her to be smart, not scared. By encouraging her to try her wings. To follow her dreams. To realize life isn't just fragile, it also moves too fast, so you have to act now. By taking time with her to drink pink tea and catch lightning bugs whenever the opportunity presents itself. By teaching her to mind your manners. To cherish your family. To love the Lord with all your heart and to know that you can have everything you think will make you safe and secure and happy in the world but you don't have anything if you don't have love."

"Amen," Hank whispered.

She threw her arms around him and kissed him.

"You left out one thing," he said softly as he searched those eyes that he had thought of every day since they had parted ways so many years ago. "We'll teach her what it means to be part of a family. Emma Newberry, will you marry me?"

"It's about time you asked again," she whispered just before she kissed him again and again, murmuring, "Yes. Yes. Yes."

Ray Bob made a mad dash inside, announcing he'd been inspired to tell Aunt Sammie how much she meant to him.

Hank settled Ruth on the bicycle to see how it felt.

Claire got out the toolbox so she could

put on the training wheels.

And Emma thanked the Lord that after following her dreams and overcoming her fears she'd finally found her answers. She had come home to stay.

Dear Reader,

Nothing prepares parents for the news that their child has a disability. Not even if they have known it since their child was born. Like Ruth in the story, my daughter's diagnosis is static encephalopathy. For her, this means that, though she has a very high IQ and gifted art ability, she has many learning disabilities along with some physical challenges. Though she struggles with things most people find simple, she has a terrific sense of humor and a good perspective.

So obviously the core of the story in *Home to Stay* is very dear to me. I wanted to get the characters of a mother and daughter right, to not make the mom a superhero and to show both her frustrations and joys. I also didn't want the child to come off as too troublesome or too sweet. And I wanted to pay homage to all the good daddies out there. Often in fiction, with a disabled child the father becomes the convenient bad guy, but the dads I know of special-needs children work multiple jobs so moms can be available for their kids or to pay for doctors or programs for their children. They do all sorts of things around the house or let those things slide because they know that there are days when meeting their child's needs takes precedence over laundry and errands and even dinner. They protect and cherish their children.

My own husband has a wonderful relationship with our daughter. She has always been his girl. When her kindergarten teacher, (who made kindergarten so tough Nat talks about it almost twenty years later), finally hung up Natalie's work the last few days of school to showcase her art as "student of the week" and she came home boasting about it, my jock of a husband had tears in his eyes. I suspect Nat will think of that teacher again when she has her first art hanging next year and I suspect my husband will tear up with pride again. I hope that I did both of them justice in *Home to Stay.*

Annie Jones

QUESTIONS FOR DISCUSSION

1. When Emma has a tough decision to make, her first inclination is to run home. Is that a choice you would also make? Why or why not?

2. Do you think that it is something more than just facing a potentially life-altering choice that propels Emma back home after a long absence? If so, what?

3. Emma has issues with her sister and feeling she doesn't measure up. Is there someone in your life that makes you feel as if you don't measure up? Have you ever considered how they might think of you, and if they perhaps feel there are many things you do better than they do?

4. Emma's daughter, Ruth, has brain injury, and Emma must choose between a certain chance to send the child to specialists and

private schools or surrounding her with family and individual attention. If you were Emma, would you have made a different choice?

5. Emma becomes worried about a stray crane on the family's pond. Do you think the crane represents more than her fears that it would draw her daughter toward a dangerous situation?

6. Hank feels that the more love surrounding a person, the stronger each relationship can be. Do you believe that? Why or why not?

7. Ruth's desire for independence centers around a bike. At what age did you learn to ride a bike and did it give you a sense of independence?

8. Hank also believes that wild animals are "God's business" and should be left alone though he is a vet who helps wounded wildlife and adopts shelter dogs. If you found a wild animal that needed aid, what would you do?

9. Emma wonders if God looks at us the way she looks at Ruth or as Hank looks at

the crane and draws her own conclusions. How do you think God looks at us?

10. Emma comes home to stay, not just for the love of Hank but for her daughter and family. In what ways do you see this enabling her to let go of some of her overprotectiveness?

11. How would you react if your child was diagnosed with a disability?

12. Do you think Emma made the right decision to turn down a marriage of security for a marriage of love? Why or why not?

13. Emma and Hank get a second chance at love. Do you know anyone who reconnected with a former flame after many years? How did it work out for them?

14. Do you think it's harder or easier to find love in a small town than a big city?

15. Did you enjoy the story? Why or why not?

ABOUT THE AUTHOR

Winner of a Holt Medallion for Southern-themed fiction, and the *Houston Chronicle*'s Best Christian Fiction Author of 1999, **Annie Jones** grew up in a family that loved to laugh, eat and talk — often all at the same time. They instilled in her the gift of sharing through words and humor, and the confidence to go after her heart's desire (and to act fast if she wanted the last chicken leg). A former social worker, she feels called to be a "voice for the voiceless" and has carried that calling into her writing by creating characters often overlooked in our fast-paced culture — from seventysomethings who still have a zest for life to women over thirty with big mouths and hearts to match. Having moved thirteen times during her marriage, she is currently living in rural Kentucky with her husband and two children.